Waiting for Mr. Benson.

The jockstrap didn't produce a second glance in a place so used to them; a sign on the wall said that the Jockstrap League of America met here once a month. A couple cowboys admired what they called my "flat golden nipples." An "Indian" liked my body with its rounded pecs. One particularly mean-looking state trooper started to come over, but a subtle shaking of my head staved him off. I leaned back against the fence and watched the game being played on the pool table. It was not pool.

I kept wondering what form the test would take. Why the Mineshaft? There was only one answer to that question; Mr. Benson intended to make this a public event. I had realized that from the beginning. My stomach felt light as I thought about all these eyes watching me now, and what they would see after Mr. Benson arrived.

MR. BENSON

JOHN PRESTON

A BADBOY BOOK

First BADBOY Edition 1992

First printing August 1992

ISBN 1-56333-041-5

Cover Photograph © 1992 Daniel Perry
Cover Design by Eduardo Andino

Manufactured in the United States of America
Published by Masquerade Books, Inc.
801 Second Avenue
New York, N.Y. 10017

ONE

Nowadays I laugh when I think of the guys in the bars who used to complain about their lovers. They talked about what a hard time they had on a weekend when their man was in a bad mood or about what marks were left once a month when they got the workout they'd been seeking for four weeks. They didn't know about masters.

They never met Aristotle Benson. He's my master, and, make no mistake about it, I am his slave.

I used to be like the others. I once had their illusions and their flightiness. When I first came out I thought *butch* was an insurance salesman in a flannel shirt. Those days, following a Paul Bunyan look-alike into an alley for a taste of piss was risky.

Mr. Benson—yes, it's always *Mister* Benson—changed all that.

I used to think men in leather and Levi's were hot numbers only for weekends. I thought life was really about working, a career, making it after a week climbing the ladder of success. Now I know that success is Mr. Benson's cock, however and whenever I can get it.

And weekends used to be sought after, as much

for relaxation as for sex. It used to be that they were for shopping, cleaning house, and brunch with friends. Now weekends are the hell I have to suffer through for Mr. Benson.

I remember when I first met him. I was twenty-five and really proud of myself. I was cocky. You know the kind: I had just been cloned and had found out that a mustache, a cute ass, and a smile with keys on the right would find me a daddy for the night. I was one of the ones who always expected the roles to be limited to the bedroom, and that breakfast would be served to me in the morning. I was proud of my looks and what I had learned they would get for me.

I'm 5'10". I was always well built. I wasn't as muscular as I am now that Mr. Benson's put me on a workout schedule he designed, but I had done some gymnastics in college and always kept in shape. I made them remember that. The jeans I wore were as tight as possible; the white cotton T-shirts, tighter. Even in winter in New York, I'd never wear more than a T-shirt under my jacket.

I even used to iron my jeans. Jeez! Get the picture? So here I'm having a beer in some pseudo-leather bar down off Christopher Street early on a Saturday night. I was horny and looking for Mr. Goodbar when in walked Mr. Benson instead.

I remember a couple of guys I had tricked with were there and I was drinking beer talking to them about their plant store when I first saw him. He was standing in a corner watching me. He wasn't smiling or glowering. He was just calmly watching me. I now know he must have been assessing me—wondering if he could bend my will and break me.

No. He wasn't wondering if he could do it; he was wondering if he wanted to do it. Mr. Benson never questions his own abilities.

He's still as handsome today as he was that night. I don't know how old he is and I've never dared ask. I do know that he's about 6'1" and that he's the most handsome man I know. He doesn't look like any model or movie star, but he is handsome. I thought then he was maybe thirty-eight. I think he looks younger than that now. So who knows?

Mr. Benson doesn't believe in preliminaries. I didn't know that then as I went through all my moves. I really did think I was dynamite in those days. I flashed my smile and showed my teeth. I made sure I stood so my ass stuck out. I made sure my jacket was open so he could see my chest and stomach through my T-shirt. Mr. Benson never blinked an eye. He never turned away. He just stood, still and aloof.

He was dressed in heavy black boots, button-fly jeans, a washed-out Levi's shirt and an old, greasy leather jacket. The jeans weren't all that tight but I could see a huge cock hanging down one side and the keys didn't look make-believe. His hair was jet black and his mustached face was rough-skinned and tanned. I was so turned on to him I could feel my dick drip. I was getting hard and was sure he'd notice. I didn't know that Mr. Benson doesn't even bother with boys' cocks. He couldn't care less.

He does care about asses. And mine was just itching for his cock to go up it. I was getting nervous. The man had been looking at me for half an hour and hadn't made a move. I used to think the "man" should make the first step, but while he hadn't left or ignored me, he didn't make any real indication that he was trying to pick me up.

I didn't know then that Mr. Benson thinks bottoms should offer themselves.

Finally, I did what I had been used to other people doing for me. I went to the bartender and gave him some money to take my nemesis a drink. Rocco knew me well, and I should have taken his advice more seriously.

"Don't do it, man. That one's too heavy for you; he's looking for more'n you have to offer."

I told him to fuck off. He got my dander up. I wasn't going to let anyone say any man was too heavy for me. And what did he mean? I was hot. I knew it. Men always told me I was becoming a good bottom. I sucked cock, I ate ass, I got slapped around, I drank piss, one guy had even gotten a fist up my ass and more than a couple had used a belt on me. A few times I had done scenes with more than one stud. They'd tied me up, they'd pissed on me, they'd shoved their jocks in my mouth. I thought I'd done it all! What a laugh! The way I was going, in five more years I still wouldn't have been ready for Mr. Benson. But he had decided he was ready for me.

I finally talked Rocco into taking him a drink. It must have been Black Label scotch; that's all Mr. Benson will drink in bars. I hope it was. If he had tasted it and it was anything else, he'd had left for sure. Rocco leaned over the bar and must have told him I bought it. He pointed at me.

Mr. Benson never changed the expression on his face. He let the glass sit.

I was getting hotter and hotter, more and more anxious and more and more horny. I know I stopped smiling. Five minutes later, he still hadn't touched his drink. I wasn't bar cruising anymore, my eyes were glued to his crotch. I remember wondering what it would smell like. I remember looking at the undone button of the bottom of his fly and asking myself if I could feel his cock if I put my fingers through there. I remember wondering what **Rocco** meant by "too heavy," and I remember sweating. Those must have been the five longest minutes in my life. Standing there thinking about his cock—was it uncut?—and waiting. The bar was starting to fill up and I was terrified that he'd find someone else to trick with.

I didn't know that Mr. Benson never just tricks.

I couldn't take it anymore. I had to talk to him before anyone else did. For one thing, I knew my act was falling apart; I knew that I was starting to fidget and move around. I was—okay, I'll admit it—such a queen that I was afraid I'd turn him off. I've learned since that nothing makes him happier than to see me uncomfortable.

I went over. His eyes watched my approach. There was no welcome in those eyes, no warmth, just their hard blue watching me. My stomach did fifteen turnovers during the fifteen steps it took me to reach him. When I finally stood in front of him I could barely force a smile. I stood frozen and must have stuttered when I finally did get out, "Hi."

He looked down at me for a minute—it must have been a full minute—and finally said, "I expect you to call me 'Sir.' If you can't manage that then there's no use in going any further."

His voice is still the same, a full booming baritone that hit me like a physical blow. I looked straight up at him. The confusion and game playing ended. Sure, there was still a part of me that was proving to Rocco that no one was too heavy for me, but what really went down was more like one of those moments when there's perfect clarity. When you know it's real, and now. *Okay, man*, I thought to myself. *Let's do it this way. Let's see what it's all about.*

At that minute I knew I hadn't been wanting to play games. All that cockiness had been testing. All those smiles and seductions I had been playing had been challenges. Someone was finally accepting my challenge. I thought, *I dare you.*

I didn't know Mr. Benson never needs a dare.

"I'm sorry, Sir, it won't happen again." It was a good moment. I don't think my voice has ever been so clear and even. I even knew not to emphasize the "Sir," it just rolled out as a natural part of the sentence. Anything else would have been mocking him.

Mr. Benson does not enjoy mockery.

He barely nodded an acknowledgment, then said, "Turn around."

I turned. Still with a little cockiness left.

"Take off your jacket."

I shucked it with my back still to him, smiling to myself and regaining some of my confidence. No one had ever *not* been impressed by this body! The appreciative eyes in the bar helped me remember that.

They're all looking at me, I thought. *A hot little stud showing a hot body to a hot man.* I loved the attention and the stares. I didn't notice Rocco's worried face. He knew. I've often wondered how. I've wondered if humpy Rocco ever stood like that in a bar, taking off his jacket in front of Mr. Benson, flexing those pumped-up arms of his, making his tattoos move around.

"Turn around."

Back to his face. So handsome. *Yeah, man, what'd you think of that!*

"You're wearing undershorts. I don't like that. And your shirt's for shit. Get into the toilet and strip off the shirt and the shorts and throw them away." It all came out in a smooth, deep tone.

I was lucky. I started to stutter a protest, but I caught myself in time. I saw his face stiffen just

10

before I started to speak. My clarity returned. *Okay, you've always wanted this. You've always wanted a real man. Don't fuck up your chance.* I stayed quiet and said, "Yes, Sir." I was surprising myself.

The kind of pride I felt as I crossed the bar to the john was a new sensation. I was showing them what I could do. I was going to display how much of a man I was. Not just a little flirt.

In the smelly, dark room I peeled off my T-shirt and pulled my jeans down over the sneakers I wore in those days. An older man taking a leak was shocked watching me strip. He stood with his mouth open. He got really shaky when I pulled my jockey shorts down and my almost full hard-on popped out, sticking straight into the air. I was hot now, wanting to get back to my man. The voyeur's Adam's apple jumped up and down like the knob of a pogo stick when I pulled my jeans up again and zipped them. I took the underwear up in my hand and nearly put it on the shelf by the door where I could get it later. *No*, I told myself. *No games.*

I realized that if I didn't enter into this fully, it wouldn't come off. Maybe I wasn't quite so stupid as I remember. I took the wadded-up cotton and tossed it into an overflowing toilet.

I walked out and back across the bar to stand in front of my new-found adversary. What would he do now? Mr. Benson didn't fail me, but then he never has. He checked my body with the appreciative eye of a wholesale butcher. I could feel him take in every little ripple of flesh. My personal transformation continued. I didn't mind this ritual; I was pleased to have finally found out why I had bothered with all those exercises. I had needed them to present a body good enough for this man's pleasure.

My nipples were almost flat in those days. They

11

were nickel-sized circles of brown flesh until Mr. Benson started to take a personal interest in their education. But still, when he reached up and his hand started to rub a thumb back and forth across their surface, it sent flashes of sensation through my whole upper torso. I forced a deep breath and unconsciously spoke: "Oh, please, Sir!"

"Please, what?" The thumb kept going back and forth. "What do you want, boy?"

My stiff cock was rubbing against the unfamiliar denim and my mind was one with that thumb as it moved over and over my chest. I couldn't find words.

"Boy, we're in trouble if a little touch to your tit is going to do this to you."

"I can take more, Sir! I want more, Sir!"

I didn't really know what that meant, but I soon found out as the thumb stopped and joined a finger to clasp the nipple tightly. I had been watching the hand's progress. When it stopped, my eyes quickly moved up to confront his. I tried to act real brave as he stared at me and started pressing harder. Slowly, his hand started twisting my soft nipple one way, then the other, each time a little further, a little harder. I was breathing through my mouth soon; the breath came in little gasps. Finally I shut my eyes to block out the growing pain.

But it felt good, too! Oh, did it ever! I kept visualizing the strong hairy forearms as they twisted my tits. Finally, I broke and carefully reached up and put my hand on Mr. Benson's forearm. I guess I just rested it there, my new consciousness telling me that any more would have been failure, that maybe I'd already failed.

He kept going. He kept pressing harder and twisting more. My face muscles contorted in pain, my mouth opened wider. I felt his nails start to dig into that tender area. My eyes reopened to see him smiling with pleasure at my pain, and, I suppose, at my taking it. My hand rested passively on the moving tendons under his warm, hairy flesh.

"Please, Sir."

There was no cockiness in that whimper. His smile broadened and he removed his short nails from my tit. A wave of relief rushed through me.

He moved his hand up to my face and gently inserted his thumb into my mouth. I started to suck on this first oral contact with him. I was greedy as my tongue bathed him inside me and grateful that his hand was in my mouth instead of on my chest.

"Boy, don't ever tell me you can take more unless you mean it, understand?"

I shook his hand up and down in agreement.

"That's good. Now, you think you've had enough, or do you think you're ready for me?" My eyes half-closed to look more directly at him. I nodded *yes* again. I was, or was ready to find out.

"That's good. Let's get a few things straight. You've been acting really prissy since I got here—showing off your ass and parading in front of all these guys. I take it you think you're hot. You aren't. You're an asshole to fuck. Nothing better. You're a piece of meat to be used however I choose. No challenges, no back-talk, no hesitations. If I want to fuck you on top of a steeple, you'll climb it."

I nodded again. His voice was talking right to my crotch.

"You do what I say with that mouth of yours, and keep it shut otherwise."

Still more nodding. By now, I was in no mood to argue with those blue eyes of his as they drilled me into the floor.

"I'm taking you to my place now." My nodding

picked up speed. He plopped his thumb out of my mouth. He reached behind his back and pulled out a pair of handcuffs. Not even watching what he was doing, he looked right at me and expertly clasped one hand.

"Turn around."

I snapped to, my arm folding behind my back as I turned; he grabbed my other hand. I didn't dare look up to see how many eyes were watching me now. I had left off performing for others and was into my own world with this man.

His hand nudged me forward. I noticed him picking up my jacket. His hand grasped my biceps and propelled me through the front door. Outside, the cool night air blew across my naked chest. I relaxed after an initial shiver. The man had taken over. No sense fighting now.

New York cab drivers have seen everything, I guess. The one Mr. Benson flagged down didn't even look twice as I was shoved into the back seat of his hack. Mr. Benson climbed in beside me and gave the driver an address on lower Fifth Avenue. I was surprised and a little frightened I perhaps had ended up in the hands of a fake. I had pegged him for Chelsea or Clinton, or maybe the East Village. But the three of us sat silently as the driver wheeled over to the appointed place. When we arrived I was even more worried. It was one of the fancy high rises that line the blocks just north of Washington Square Park. A very friendly, very big, very black doorman was waiting. He pulled open the door.

"Evenin', Mr. Benson. Got yourself a hot one, huh?" The massive uniformed male beamed down on me. I couldn't believe it as he reached in and pulled me out onto the sidewalk while Mr. Benson paid the fare and finally stepped out himself. (But it was the first time I heard his name. I made sure I didn't forget it.)

"Yes. Time for a little fresh meat, Tom." I may have been ready for Mr. Benson, but I wasn't ready for the late-night strollers approaching us. I was more than a little relieved when they led me into the building lobby and right into the elevator. I was to learn that Mr. Benson was a wealthy man. Even without the wealth he probably couldn't have cared less what people thought of him.

We silently rode the elevator to the top floor.

"Have a nice night, now." The doorman smiled as he reached for the gate. I had expected to walk into a corridor and, already grateful for not having met any other tenants, hoped none would suddenly show up now. But the gate revealed a door which Mr. Benson used his own key to unlock. I was about to enter my first real penthouse in New York City.

Mr. Benson's apartment, of course, wasn't full of Bloomingdale's shit. His style was more California ranch house. A large fireplace dominated the space; rugs over bare wood floors, and stucco walls. Sliding glass doors led to a terrace. I wasn't invited to look at views; this is not a lesson on butch interior decorating.

Mr. Benson wasn't in the mood to give me a guided tour. He left me standing in the doorway while he walked over and lit the firewood. When it was well started he stood and turned to face me. He smiled, as though he were pleased I was so vulnerable. What had he expected? I was half-naked, cold, and slightly shivering with my wrists cuffed behind me and my mind still reeling over the trip from the bar to his apartment. The mind-set of subservience which I had begun to assume had almost left. He brought it back.

He took off his leather jacket and tossed it over

mine on the couch. Then he went to a large leather chair near the fire and dropped himself down, all the while smiling at me. He spread his long legs and kneaded the bulge. He pumped up enough hard manhood to remind me why I was there.

"Come here, boy."

When I stood in front of him, his eyes motioned for me to kneel. His foot spread my knees when I went down between his legs, looking deep into his crotch. I worked to taste his heat again.

His deep voice started again. "Now, boy, you're here to suck cock, aren't you?" I nodded gently.

"You're going to do it good, boy?"

Oh yes, Sir! My mind started its acrobatics. Was it cut? Would there be skin for my tongue to play with? Would it be clean or full of cheese? I wanted to know. My head dove down, ignoring the strong hand which pressed the cloth hard against my nose. He kept me just a few inches from the buttons of his Levi's. I moaned right out loud when I was stopped short of my goal.

His hand drew back and quickly, sharply, savagely slapped my face.

"Who ordered you to go for that yet?"

What the fuck…

"You wait till you earn that cock."

I nearly yelled out.

"Do you want to earn that cock, boy?" His voice slid down to an even more deepballed register.

"Yes, Sir!" I said smartly.

"What'll you do for that cock, boy?" His hand left my mouth free to respond this time. My jaws formed words.

"I'll suck it, Sir." My voice was muffled but the words came out and every breath brought with it more of the sharp, sweet air.

"Anyone'll do that."

"I'll eat your ass, Sir…"

"…and?"

"I'll suck your balls, Sir…"

"…and?"

"I'll drink your piss, Sir…"

"…and?"

"I'll clean your boots, Sir…"

"…and?"

"I'll lick your whole body, Sir."

"…and?"

"I'll give you my ass, Sir…"

"Come on, boy, come up with something real. Any fairy will do those things for me." My sexual euphoria was petering out and my imagination was going with it. What more could I offer? I knew I had a lot to learn. I had just put more into words than I had ever dared. Mr. Benson was definitely going to de-clone me!

I looked up, taking my eyes away from his crotch for the first time. My chest was heaving. I sweated from the warmth of the fire. I met his eyes and said the words: "I'll be your slave, Sir."

He smiled like a proud schoolteacher. "That's right, boy, you'll be my slave."

It wasn't the man's crotch that sent my stomach reeling now. It was the *intensity* of those words as we exchanged them. They were real. They were hard.

He leaned back in his chair and unbuttoned his pants. He reached in and pulled out a handful of hairy balls and a big, fat cock.

"Now, don't you dare touch these, boy; look at my cock and balls and study them. Think what they'd taste like, how your nose'd feel rubbed down in there, how good the skin would be against your lips. What your tongue would taste. But you touch my meat before I let you…"

17

The last word was strung out so long it was a sentence unto itself. I had figured out by now that these dares weren't to be tested. I sat on my haunches and watched Mr. Benson get a hard-on.

His cock filled slowly without any extra help. It filled up with thick purple veins weaving around the shaft, growing up the pole, and slowly disappearing into his full foreskin.

Mr. Benson was uncut.

His foreskin covered his prick, with only a pink slit showing over the folds, bunched on top. The cock kept growing till it was hard and then it started to jump up in little jerks when it reached his belt. I have never wanted anything as badly as I wanted to taste the cheese on the shaft of Mr. Benson's cock.

"Look good?"

"Yes, Sir!"

"Why isn't your tongue hanging out?" I took his question as an order. Breathing through my mouth made me look like a panting dog. That's okay. I was. Hot drool trickled down the sides of my mouth.

A popper snapped. I quickly took my eyes from his cock. I was terrified of breaking his commandment. I looked down at his balls just as the new rush pushed inside my head.

It was a grave mistake. Cocks may rule a lot of people, both the ones who have them and those who want them. But if any part of Mr. Benson's body is worth worshiping—and most of it is—his balls are the most deserving. They're heavy ovals pulling down on a nearly hairless, silky-looking sac. The weight stretches the skin taut across their surface; small, dark, purple/red lines crisscross their flesh. The skin folds luxuriously back up to the same place his cock begins.

I have never ever needed poppers to worship Mr. Benson's balls.

The amyl tried to take over. I was in a frustrated ecstasy of pleasure, my tongue hanging out, my spit flowing down my chin, my new master's cock and balls on an altar of denim in front of me. I knew I could touch. I shouldn't touch. I wanted to follow orders. I wanted to deserve all this. I wanted to taste. I wanted to obey. I was confused. I was stopped short in my mind. Slowly, slowly, I started to weep in frustration, salty tears flowing down to join my spit. I was turning into a cockworshiping animal.

"Now we start, boy."

Mr. Benson meant business.

I wept softly. The tears carried away every single vestige of pride I had left. Mr. Benson loved it. He chuckled softly and put his warm hand up to the side of my face. His strokes patted my head as I pushed against this first loving contact.

"Lick my balls. Only my balls."

I went more slowly this time, pressing my face softly at first, taking in the sweet odor of stale piss and sweat and putting my tongue meekly against the sac, taking a tentative taste, then again, and a third time. Soon I was slurping the eggs. I bent my whole body for each movement.

"Good boy. Now lick my cock. Just lick. Just lick the shaft. Don't put it in your mouth."

My lips moved up and traced those thick veins, beginning at the ball skin, going up in three-inch moves. Each time I got to the peak, I'd drop back and start up again. My whole body wanted to suck in that cock, but there was something else happening now: Mr. Benson was turning on! His prick was bobbing up and down as I worked on it. I know Mr. Benson loves that now; I know he'd let me do it for an hour at a time, but that night I guess we were both caught up in the moment 'cause next thing I knew his big hands worked me up from the floor.

"Stand up!"

As soon as I was upright, he popped my jeans and pulled them down to my ankles. He remained in the chair. Now he slipped back into the seat and said, "My boots, asshole."

My jeans bound my ankles as effectively as the cuffs bound my wrists. I dropped down on my knees again and leaned over, resting my open mouth on the rough leather. My mind flipped into acrobatics again, changing my whole view of myself and this man. The cocky clone of two hours ago was disappearing. Now I was earning it! Earning everything I was going to get that night, the next day, the next month…I was working for it! The real thing!

Mr. Benson moved my face over to the next boot.

There were no words. None were necessary.

My thoughts traveled in ways I never would have predicted. All I wanted right then was to have this man wearing the best-looking boots in New York. I wanted him to be proud of how each one gleamed with the care I was putting in cleaning them. I was polishing them with my own spit; I rinsed them with my own tongue.

He pulled my head up. I nearly fought again; I wasn't finished! But he was pleased. He spit full in my face to prove it. I didn't have a chance to enjoy that; he pivoted me around a full half circle and pushed me flat on my face again. The rough wool rug wasn't nearly as inviting as his boots.

His foot spread my knees as far apart as the binding jeans would allow. It reached in between the legs and pulled my ass straight up in the air until my shoulders and neck were my only support. The boot kneaded my balls, played with my cock and finally began rubbing up and down the naked crack of my ass. Each time it passed my asshole, I couldn't help but shudder at the vulnerable contact.

Suddenly the shiny leather was gone and I heard and felt Mr. Benson as he leaned over, spit on my hole and cracked my cheek all in one movement. I started, but knew not to move. He began a deep, slow conversation with my ass, punctuated with increasingly sharp blows on the flesh.

"Pretty hole, waiting for daddy to fill it…"

Crack!

"…waiting for his big cock…"

Slap!

"…hungry for his fist…"

Bang!

"…wants to suck his come…"

Smack!

"…drink his piss…"

Mr. Benson stood and walked around to face my side. He stuck his boot back in my face. My mouth opened, grateful for the diversion from my rear still sticking in the air. But I knew what the movement of cloth above me meant and couldn't help but groan in anticipation of the cutting whirl of his belt as it streaked down to mark my offered body. My groan grew to a cry as I heard his arm pull the belt back up and again speed the leather back down to my ass. I desperately gnawed at his boot, knowing he couldn't feel it, but hoping I could stop myself from feeling the welts growing as the black line left its red imprint again…and again…and again.

I couldn't believe that my ass was still in the air when he finally finished. My mouth still silently worked on his boot; the only sound in the room was our heaving breaths.

"Pretty ass, baby." You could almost hear him smile. "And it's never looked better."

He took the boot away from me and went back to his chair. My butt burned, but my hole was open to the cool air. I heard him rummaging through something behind me. Then I felt a damp hand at once cool on my cheeks and warm on my hole. The hand was damp with grease. He moved into me first by one finger; he added a second and then a third. He massaged me expertly. He loosened the remaining resistance of my already defeated ring and slowly brought his thumb and final finger in. He pushed against the little wall I had left. I felt his knuckles glide in after them. I let out a slight moan as I felt myself gratefully embrace his squared fist.

We stayed joined like that for a while. My body was in Mr. Benson's grip, he feeling my whole being. He knelt down finally and, staying behind me, pushed further into me. I couldn't help but groan with each thrust.

I heard him pumping his cock as he probed me. I listened as his inhaling picked up speed to keep pace with his fast-moving foreskin. I wanted that cock so badly. I had worked so hard for it. But I guess I knew I had won more than just his cock and I was content to grip harder on his forearm and feel its hairs tickle me as he pumped, and he pumped until finally the hot rush of his come came showering over my back.

His hand withdrew from me almost as slowly and carefully as it had entered. I felt a sudden emptiness. I raised up to a kneel and shook my head to clear it. I sat back on my haunches, still with my back to him. The confusion of emotions inside me went from defeat to elation, with fatigue overriding them all. I closed my eyes, hoping to rest.

Mr. Benson wasn't finished. "Turn around!"

I turned and finally faced him again. A towel had appeared and he was wiping his arm. His smile was satisfied, I hoped. "You're a good piece of ass." He finished with the towel and tossed it to the floor. He stood and once again his cock and those beautiful balls were in front of me. How did I ever get the strength to turn on again? He reached over behind me and undid the handcuffs. I brought my sore wrists in front of me and rubbed them gratefully.

His cock bobbed in my eyes. "You want to beat off?"

"Yes, Sir." My voice was something less than a whisper.

His hand offered his cock to my lips. I took in the silky half-flaccid tool. My eyes went to his and saw his pleasure at the scene as I worked my own prick. My tongue went around the pole, my mind concentrating once again on this essence of my man's being.

I should have expected it. What else could he have been planning?

"Spill one drop and you're going to be in big trouble." The flow began weakly, the salty, acidic fluid easily pouring down my throat. He had picked up his belt again and was laying it on my bare shoulders. He was taunting me! He would have loved nothing more than such an easy excuse to use that leather on my back, just the way he had on my ass. The piss came more quickly and grew into a gush. I swallowed as fast as I could to get all of the golden liquid down, drinking this man-water just as I had embraced his arm. I wanted him in my guts. I wanted to please him. I wanted to escape the punishment that would have come from the slightest infraction of his rules.

The flow receded back to a trickle. He probably was disappointed in one way that I had taken all of that, all the piss he could pump into me at once, but his eyes betrayed another emotion. The fucker was proud of me! He was proud that I had taken all his piss, his fist, his beatings, his ego. I had become a prized possession. I could feel it.

He lifted me to my feet and embraced me. I stepped out of my jeans while he quietly went around and turned off the lights. Then he led me to one of the closed doors and opened it to reveal a perfectly masculine bedroom, one dominated by a king-sized bed sheathed with black leather, whose odor filled the air. There were a couple leather-upholstered chairs off to one side, and large, heavy wooden dressers. There was still another set of windows with another beautiful view.

My mind felt the soothing sheets envelop me while his strong body lay beside me. My neck longed as much for the large pillow under the spread as it did for the strength of his arm around me. My ass waited for a comforting mattress as much as it did his stroking hand. I wanted to sleep with my face turned in his sweaty armpit.

Mr. Benson went over to a closet and opened it. He pulled out a large form I couldn't figure out. He tossed it to the corner of the room nearest me. "Sleep there. You've a long day ahead of you tomorrow." And he walked over to that thronelike bed and crawled—alone—between its heavy covers. I was stunned, but I went over to my corner and spread the sleeping bag out on the floor. I crawled in and closed my eyes. This is how I should have expected to spend my first night in Mr. Benson's house.

TWO

Mr. Benson kicked me awake the next morning. The kick wasn't really hard or vicious, but I knew it was a kick and not a nudge. My eyes opened at the sudden disturbance and found those wonderful balls hanging over my face. Those beautiful eggs were pressing towards me as if they were waiting for a good morning kiss.

Mr. Benson, though, wasn't in a romantic mood. "Get up, asshole, I'm going to shower. You make breakfast. Eggs: sunnyside up; bacon: crisp; coffee: black. I eat in the dining room."

Off he went as I stretched against the confining sleeping bag. My morning yawn helped me discover the tender spots on my ass where his belt had left what I knew would be black and blue marks. Still, I felt good this morning. What I really wanted was to curl up in the sleeping bag and play with my piss hard-on, but the sudden whoosh of the shower in the bathroom reminded me that the kick in my side and the growled orders meant that last night's rules weren't to be forgotten.

I jumped up naked and went into the enormous living room. I crossed the islands of carpet toward the dining area. The kitchen would obviously be behind the door at the head of the bulky, dark wood table. I pushed against the spring hinge and found myself in the midst of spotless gleaming-white tiles and stainless steel.

It took a five-minute game of hide and seek for utensils before I could even begin the bacon frying, and start the toast and coffee.

I was too far from the bathroom to have heard the shower turn off; I jumped a foot when I heard his voice boom from the table: "Coffee!"

No explanation was needed or offered. I found a mug and poured out the first cup from the freshly dripped pot. I pushed back through the door and found my new man seated, wearing a heavy flannel bathrobe, already a few pages into the Sunday *Times*.

I put the coffee down beside him and couldn't help but marvel at how handsome he was with his thick hair wet and matted from the shower. His mustache looked even fuller than I had remembered, now that it stood out against the smooth-shaven skin. His clean odor—there was no after-shave—was one of the best morning smells I could imagine.

Last night flashed before me. I thought of my new experience of being with this man—who took what he wanted how he wanted it, but who had, in his own way, also shown pride and affection. I smiled as a wave of warmth went through my groin. I quickly went back to the kitchen.

Five minutes later, I carried his breakfast through the door. He barely nodded as I placed it in front of him and left him silverware. I went back to the kitchen and brought out the coffeepot and refilled his cup. Still, he only gave me grudging notice as he plowed through the newspaper. I was foolish enough to have expected more. I've learned since then to expect nothing from Mr. Benson; that way I appreciate what I get.

I finally got some notice from him when I came back to the table a third time, now carrying my own breakfast plate. I had pulled out the chair to his right and had begun to sit down when his voice bellowed out and caught me a foot from the seat. "Don't you *dare!*"

"Sir?" I was so surprised, my voice was almost a squeak.

"Don't you dare use the furniture in this house. No slave's ass has ever touched furniture in my home! On the floor, stupid; remember your place and go over and eat on the floor!"

He pointed to the corner to his right. Bewildered, angry—and probably hurt—I took the plate and went over to the corner. His eyes were furious in their emphasis. He wasn't playing, he meant it. I was not going to use the furniture. The games—did I still think they were games?—weren't going to end just because it was Sunday morning. His arm and pointing finger didn't relax until I had taken my assigned place.

My humiliation had almost erased my appetite. I crouched with my plate on my lap and buried myself in a whole new series of emotions. Just a few minutes ago I had been happy to be cooking for my new man, proud of the body he had appreciated so much the night before, cocky of the muscles that had taken so much of his abuse, and anticipating an afternoon lounging around the house, hopefully having sex again.

Now I felt like shit. The odor of body sweat trapped in a sleeping bag all night, the pain of the welts covered with his come, and the unattractiveness of a day's growth of beard joined with the shame of eating naked on the floor. I remember those intense feelings well. I sometimes wonder why I didn't leave right then, I was so angry with the bastard.

But I know why I didn't leave. Because just then, when the feelings were so intense, I looked up and saw that Mr. Benson's robe had parted open. He was reaching down and lazily scratching his groin. I watched as his hand pulled away and his balls nestled back down on the chair and his cock drooped over them, it too resting on the seat.

There it was, the reason I had come here last night—his crotch, with its dark mane of pubic hair, its protective thighs beside it. All the tastes and feels and arousals came back. For five years now, whenever I wonder why I've stayed, all I have to do is remember that cock and balls.

I got my breakfast down. I finally decided, what the hell. He wants me on the floor, I'll stay on the floor, and I ate a hearty meal. I took my plate back to the kitchen and then cleared his place so he could spread out his papers. His coffee cup was empty. I decided if I was going to do this, I might as well do it right, so I reheated the coffee and filled his cup for him, then went in and did the dishes.

Standing over the sink, I realized for the first time just how enormous his apartment was. My whole flat would have fit into the large living room. And I thought, really for the first time, how wealthy he must be. I wondered who he was when he wasn't playing topman.

After I dried the last plate, I was at a loss what to do. Shower? Get dressed? I just didn't know what he expected or wanted. I tried to anticipate: what does a slave do when he hasn't been given any orders? That's what I was now, a slave. I had said the words myself last night, he had accepted it. So, what do I do?

Finally I came to the inevitable conclusion. I obviously wasn't going to sit up at the table and read the paper, I didn't presume to use his bathroom to take a shower, I wasn't supposed to dress. So, I went back into the dining room, sat back down in my corner, damned my luck when I saw that his robe had been pulled shut, and I went back to sleep.

Mr. Benson must have found that acceptable. When I had gone back into the room, he was only halfway through the main body of the paper; when I opened my eyes again, he was just finishing the last section. Mr. Benson reads his Sunday *Times* carefully, and I know now that that meant at least an hour had passed. When he finished the last page, he pushed back in his chair, threw his arms up in the air and did a long, leisurely stretch, his body touching only the back of the chair with his spine and the floor with the tips of his toes. This time when the robe came open, his whole torso was in view. The sight of the hair-covered physique gave me an instant erection.

When his yawn was done, he collapsed into the seat. Scratching his balls, he smiled over at me. "Come here, boy."

I jumped up and went over beside him. He reached up and pulled my neck down. "Suck my tit."

I was amazed at this awareness that I was even present, and at his sudden sexual energy. I bent over and took his heavy pec in my mouth and sucked smoothly. One hand kept pulling on my neck and the other went to his own cock. He started pumping himself while he purred into my ear, "Nice boy...that's right...suck on daddy's tit...use that tongue."

He didn't mind when I reached up and took his pectoral muscle in my hand, pushing its heavy flesh up into my face and rubbing its thick hair against my skin. The pointed red nipple in my mouth hardened against my rubbing tongue. I was almost—but not quite—forgetting his rigid cock, not more than two feet from my mouth, stretching against his fist.

"Suck, boy, make Mr. Benson feel real good... work for him...make him come, yeah...make him shoot his load while you suck his tit..."

His hand pushed harder against my neck. I could see his stomach tense and begin to heave, tight lines creasing his muscular belly. "Work on it, asshole..." His voice came louder. "Suck on it!" His fist was flying and a sudden wad of come shot out and slammed against my chin, and another, and a third fell short and landed on his stomach, then more poured out of his cock, down over his dark pubic hair.

I stood, still bent over him, softly nibbling his nipples for a short while. When his breathing became regular again, he pushed my face down from his chest. "Lick it off."

My tongue lashed out down the trail of body hair, vacuuming up the deposits of semen, licking up the clear salty fluid that had been foamy white only seconds ago. I knelt and got closer to his softening cock and sucked on his groin hair, cleaning it small strands at a time. I'd suck on clumps and pull them straight up from his body where they'd stand with my wetness. Once again, I longed for his cock. But by then I knew not to take it without permission.

Finally, he stood. "Good boy." He patted my head. "Go take a shower. I left a towel out for you, and a razor. Be quick. I want to talk to you."

I jumped up with my hard-on bobbing up and down in front of my stomach. No use trying to cover it, I thought. Only twenty-four hours ago I would have been embarrassed by this hard-on, squeamish about how my body was being used and exposed, but Mr. Benson had made me forget about all that. I realized I should be naked; my body should be used this way by a man obviously superior to me. Did I really believe that, that Mr. Benson was my superior?

I thought about it under the warm flow of the shower. Everything in my background denied the idea that any man was better than any other. But I wondered about myself now; my bland middle-class background's values were too obvious when placed in the context of this man's lifestyle. Funny how class will tell even through leather and jeans. There was something obviously classy about Mr. Benson, more than the implied wealth. And, for the first time, I realized there was something obviously bourgeois about myself. In another time and place I would really have been this man's slave.

The thought came while I was shaving. I stood there and fantasized Mr. Benson a sheik and myself the Arab boy whose life depended on my master's whim. My cock shot straight up against the cold porcelain of the sink.

As I wiped the last of the shaving cream from my face, I had visions of Mr. Benson the Norseman and me the English peasant he'd just kidnapped to take back to Vikingland for God-knows-what sort of nightmarish existence.

I was beating off by the time Mr. Benson had become a Turkish potentate…I, a captured yeoman from the Crusaders' armies, standing in front of him while he decided whether or not to turn me into a eunuch. I shot straight in the air as he decided no, that there were better ways to use me.

I know now there was something very serious about what was going through my mind. I was seriously considering who I was in relationship to this man. There was nothing that had happened that led me to believe for a second that this was a potential "boyfriend" or "lover" in any sense that I had experienced. The differences were too obvious and they were stacked all in his favor. The only thing I had going for me was a body he had evidently found attractive, coupled with my willingness to let him use it to make him happy. If I needed fantasies to justify the degradation and humiliation he would demand, then let them be. I was deciding that Mr. Benson was the man I wanted to love. If class and money and age were going to separate us, I would use my sexuality and a willingness to be powerless to overcome them. I would be a slave in order to love this man.

The real decision was made when I walked, clean and refreshed, into the main room and saw him. He couldn't have heard my bare feet and he didn't look up as I stood there in the doorway, mesmerized by the vision of manhood I thought the most perfect I could ever imagine.

The fireplace had been lit, the burning logs casting a warm glow from inside the marble front that dominated the room. Mr. Benson sat in a red-brown leather chair just to the left of the fireplace, his leg casually thrown over the chair's arm. He was reading a book, its binding old and worn-looking; a Brandenburg Concerto was playing on the stereo. It might seem strange that he looked perfectly dressed in a T-shirt and old, worn jeans, but it was perfect. The room, the setting, the fire joining the light of a single reading lamp against a gray New York winter sky; the clothes and the casualness of it all had in common a perfect masculinity.

I was torn between wanting to take all this in and wanting to demonstrate my emotions. The need to act took over. I went to him and dropped full length on the floor, spreading my willingness to be sacrificed before him. I reached my head over and lightly kissed the bare foot once, then again, and again until I finally took the biggest toe into my mouth and passively sucked on it. Just like that: spread out, feeling the front of my body pressed against the rough wool, my head resting on its side on the floor sucking the one part of my man's body that seemed appropriate.

I stared at his feet. They were large. The skin on the bottom was roughly callused, the top perfectly proportioned. I was so close I could trace the thick veins that stood out just like the ones on his cock. I could see delicate lines of smaller blood vessels. I could watch the throbbing of the artery above his heel. I could count the hairs that grew sparsely over the top of his foot: Mr. Benson's foot, my master's foot.

After a few minutes of ecstasy he pulled the toe away and rubbed the tips of all five digits back and forth across my slightly opened mouth, running the toenails against my teeth.

Then, slowly, he changed the pattern and brought the soles of his feet up to cover my lips, and grated the worn skin against my mouth. Each swing he would press down harder, forcing my mouth further open until my jaws were pried apart, my neck against the floor. He forced me to turn over on my back with subtle manipulations of my head with his feet. My arms were spread over my head, my legs angled open beneath my once-again hard cock, resting, pulsating on my belly.

Mr. Benson's next words shocked me. I never suspected he would say, "You better go home now."

My eyes must have shown my bewilderment, but he added nothing more.

"Have I done something wrong, Sir?"

"No, you haven't done anything wrong. I'm just not sure about you. And I'm not convinced you know about yourself. You see, boy, I'm not into playing a lot of games with some little "disco doll" who thinks he might be into SM. If I'm going to bother investing in one person, I want to know it's going to be worth my time; it's not enough that the other person is getting off on it. You—you've wanted these experiences, but what are you going to give me in return?"

My ears were still burning with embarrassment over the disco doll phrase. Disco doll! Give him in return! "What do you want, Sir?"

"Everything. That's the point. Everything. I want control...of the situation and of you. I want your body whenever I want it without any crap from your head. I want obedience, sex, and loyalty. I want someone here who has no allegiance to anything but me. You're not that person. You'd still be looking, probably. You'll get back to the attitude you had last night. You haven't had the experience to know better...and I'm not in the business of being a teacher."

My fantasies evaporated. He was going to put me out. Just like that. Into the street. Back to the bar. I stayed lying on the floor and looked him straight in the eye. "How can I prove myself to you? How can I show you that I understand what you're saying, Sir? That I want to make a commitment to you?

"Last night taught me more about myself than I ever thought I knew. It's shown me what makes me happy, what I've been missing. I know it's only been one night, but one night can mean everything. I'll gladly give up what I have to, to be with you on your terms. I need to be with you. After this, everything else will seem like...it's artificial."

Something I had said, or how I had said it, set Mr. Benson off. He looked thoughtfully for a while and

34

then finally spoke. "I still want you to go. Go home, think it over...and when you are very sure, call me. But know that when you call me—if you do—that I'm going to put you through a test that will be worse than your worst vision of hell. Know that if you call me, I'll expect unquestioning service from you. I'll expect you to be mine—not a trick, not a lover, not a person—just a piece of ass who happens to be my personal servant. No games, no breaks, no headaches. My pleasure, my timing, my rules."

I stayed there, my cock so rigid from his words I thought I'd shoot all over myself right then and there. Mr. Benson went back to his book and soon I got up and went to get dressed. When I came back to him, he handed me a piece of paper. I took it, determined to keep myself together, and silently followed him to the elevator door and waited for the cage to arrive.

The operator was not the same man as the night before and he was mercifully silent on the way down. I needed quiet to sort out my thoughts about the glorious man I had just left. Was the one night all he had to offer? No, the control he had exerted this morning had shown more. Was he just being kind and letting me down easy by sending me home? No, he wouldn't have left me the option of returning if that were the case, and I had to treat him with trust, I knew that. The whole thing had to be dealt with with trust and respect or none of it would work.

Call him when I'm sure, he had said. I should have stopped at a pay phone then and there. But I knew he wanted me to think about it all and decide. I'll do that, all right. The one thing I needed to think and decide about quickly was the threat of a "test." The belt marks on my ass showed me that something planned by Mr. Benson, some test, would be nothing to take lightly. Was I really ready for that; was he worth *anything*? And was he really so special that it was worth never again looking at another man?

Just in time to answer my question, I walked right into the oncoming figure of Larry. I was so deep in thought I never had the chance to lessen my pace even a slight bit. Larry was the omnipresent flannel-shirt-Levi's stud in every bar in New York. Hulking, tall Larry, now, as always, in full uniform: construction boots, bomber jacket, flannel shirt, button-fly jeans with two buttons open to show a flash of jockstrap. The light brown mustache completed the image of every clone on Christopher Street. But hot, he was very hot. Larry, whom I'd wanted every time I'd seen him, who had always smiled, but never responded to me sexually.

"Look where the hell you're going!"

"Sorry, Larry."

"Hey, guy, almost didn't recognize you." He smiled gleaming teeth at me and slapped my shoulder in greeting. The small talk continued as I tried to focus on him instead of the memory of Mr. Benson. When I had, finally, it dawned on me that after a year of cruising him in the bars, Larry was interested in me. A godsend! A fucking godsend! Here was my test. Would I turn on to Larry like I had to Mr. Benson?

I perked up, flashed my teeth back at his, slouched to show ass, nonchalantly opening my jacket to show bare skin under the brown leather. He like that—a lot. The not-so-subtle invitation to his apartment followed quickly.

It was a good test. Good because Larry pretty soon had my attention. Good because I found myself impressed by this bar-god. Maybe Mr. Benson was right; if I could change over so quickly, maybe I really wasn't ready. I think about the encounter, five years ago, often. What if it had been different? I was only twenty-five then. What if I hadn't ended up with Mr. Benson?

But those are idle thoughts. I did end up with Mr. Benson. And I know now that Larry was a big part of the decision.

Mr. Benson lived on lower Fifth Avenue. Larry lived in Chelsea. According to my values, they equaled each other. Mr. Benson's lifestyle of affluence versus Larry's life as king of the gay ghetto. But I couldn't keep them on a par for long. As soon as I walked into Larry's cramped one-bedroom apartment, I knew he'd have been better off if he hadn't tried at all. The furniture was supposed to look imported—it did, like it had just been unloaded off a boat from Korea. The carpet was strictly K-Mart, and the prints on the walls were every clichéd reproduction of Utrillo, Gauguin, and Rembrandt that had ever made the original artists spin in their graves. Poor Larry. Poor me!

My first hint of Larry's lifestyle had to combat the most perfect part of Mr. Benson's.

The obligatory joint was lit. I had a hard time adjusting to sitting on a couch. Larry's conversation compounded the sin of his accoutrements; he was proud of them. The colors, he offered, went well with one another. None of those colors went well with anything.

I longed for Larry to start. I guess Mr. Benson had already taught me to let the top begin. But when he started to light the second joint, I had had it. My hand went to his crotch and opened more buttons to expose the whole of that oft-glimpsed jockstrap.

I cupped the crusted mound and got an erection thinking about burying my face in it. Larry was already breathing hard.

"Not here. In the bedroom."

I followed him through the one door and tried not to wince at the fringed curtains and matching ribbed cotton bedspread. I tossed myself on the bed, trying to keep hard with thoughts of that wonderful jock in my mouth when Larry began to undress. Undress? Himself?

"You, too."

I shrugged. I had only my jacket, jeans, socks and sneakers left after last night. They came off quickly. Larry stood clad in only the jockstrap. He blew up his chest in pride and waited obviously for an appreciative remark. I had never been so disappointed in my life!

All the flannel and denim had hidden an almost hairless body with wan, pale skin. The flesh was firm, but there was no definition to any of the layers. I knew this was going to be a trial. I had never expected that part of the function of all his uniform clothing was to be a girdle.

He came over and lay on top of me, his vapid flesh cool to the touch. He kissed me; the kiss felt strange on lips that had just come from worshiping Mr. Benson's tough, callused feet.

I tried. God knows I tried to get into the spirit of the whole thing. I ground my groin up to meet the jockstrap that by now was his only redeeming virtue. But he missed so badly. His every move compared negatively to Mr. Benson in every way.

"What can I do for you, Sir?"

"No 'Sir.'" Larry pulled himself up. "None of that role playing shit. We're both men."

Momentarily I was puzzled, but I soon realized what that meant as his lips came down to rejoin mine in one of those blubbering kisses of his. My cock drooped as I thought it over: the uniform, the jockstrap, him grinding away on top of me, but I bet...I bet...I reached down to his large ass and tentatively poked a finger into the hidden hole. The loud moan was proof enough.

"Just buddies, man...real buddies...be a buddy, man...stick it in...fuck your buddy, man..."

I pulled away as violently as if I were drowning in his waves of flesh, my then-flaccid cock bobbing out from his thighs' clutches.

"Sorry, man, I got to go to the john."

The oldest line in gaydom allowed me to escape panting into the toilet. Once safely inside, I closed the door and sat on the bowl and tried to collect my thoughts about this idol turned bottom and my reactions.

A world of flannel clones living in Chelsea walkups was the alternative to Mr. Benson? I think the deciding factor was my glancing over to the sink and seeing a bar of soap sitting there proudly, wearing a Bloomingdale's trademark. No, this was not a substitute for Mr. Benson. I tested this theory a little more by standing up and opening the medicine chest. Hairspray, Brut, Macho cologne...I had suspected they would be there, but the evidence really made me recoil.

By now my cock was less than flaccid; it had shriveled. I quickly went into the bedroom and put on my clothes, Larry watching me as he smoked a cigarette.

"So you're really into all that top/bottom shit."

I suddenly realized that this was the first time he could have seen the marks on the back of my body. He had probably figured it out even without their witness, given how I'd been reacting.

"Yeah, I guess so," I lied as I tied my sneakers.

"Poor little fairy, doomed to look for a knight on a black charger for the rest of your life. Don't you know there are no real masters in gay life?"

"No, I don't know that, Larry." I looked him straight in the eye.

"There are only make-believers. You settle for the closest you can get with that."

"I'm not willing to do that, Larry. I believe there are some men able enough to give as men and some able enough to take as men. I'm only twenty-five; I'm going to keep trying to give and trying to find some-one man enough to take."

"Pretty little fool, go ahead. You're young; go ahead and try. No one's going to blame you for try-ing. But everyone you know will say 'we told you so' when you come back."

I didn't even respond. I just left. Quickly going down the stairs and onto Eighth Avenue, I real-ized I wasn't fleeing; I was just leaving behind a sad figure who tried to hide his own feelings by his criticism of me.

It was cold on the street. I missed my T-shirt as the wind off the river blew into my jacket. I rushed home to my own Chelsea apartment, only a few blocks from Larry's. Loud disco music blared a welcome through the doorway. I nearly collapsed in a sigh.

"Oh, shit." It just slipped out, under my breath.

I opened the door and walked through a cloud of marijuana smoke. Jimmy and someone who was obviously a trick were sitting in the sparse living room. Our limited resources had mercifully kept us from any pretensions of style. At least here it was honestly comfortable.

I used to like Jimmy a lot in those days. I wanted to tell him everything about the evening. The hot man, hot sex, and fantasy mingling with reality. At first he and his friend just looked at me through glazed eyes. They did perk up at the mention of the penthouse. Their wide-eyed interest turned to mild repulsion when I described the piss-drinking climax to the evening.

"I wish gay people would stop degrading themselves," Jimmy exclaimed.

"But it wasn't really degrading, Jimmy. I mean, it was *him* I was drinking. It was like, like...a communion. It was his water, man. His gift."

"You're sick," the new friend chimed in. "How could you?"

"What did it taste like?" Jimmy owned up to a little more interest.

"I really don't want to hear about it," the friend interrupted. "Some things are best left to wharves and back rooms."

"Though it *was* in a penthouse," Jimmy cautioned.

"Well...the rich are always the most perverted. They can't deal with their power."

"Mr. Benson can!" I defended.

"What's his name?" Jimmy asked.

"Mr. Benson," I repeated.

"But his first name?"

I didn't know. I took out the paper with the telephone number.

"Aristotle Benson," I read.

They laughed. I was struck by how apt it was: Aristotle, teacher of young men.

I quickly gave up telling my story. I went into my own room, barely keeping the departure civil. I lay back on my unmade bed and thought. I looked around at the disheveled room, the centerfolds from *Drummer* the only wall decorations; the Christopher Street drag, really no better than Larry's, was the only clothing visible. I thought about the one suit hanging in the closet for work tomorrow. An insurance company.

A picture of my family was on the bureau. My

family lived a thousand miles away in a Midwestern backwater. I wasn't alienated from them, but I was leading a life so different that only distance could be the result.

Larry and Jimmy were leading lives as alienated as my family's.

Mr. Benson was the only person to kindle emotional flames in me, flames of passion and intensity that brought a warm hope for security and knowledge.

I felt trapped. Sunday. What can you do at this time of day on Sunday? The Ramrod! New York's favorite weekend leather bar would be hot even this early.

I jumped into a full set of clothes. A little heavier this time, I thought. Okay, the construction boots and a black T-shirt I had been a little leery of wearing before. That seemed better. I ran out of the apartment without a good-bye and caught a cab at the corner.

The Ramrod was as full of men as I had hoped. They formed a veritable sea of black leather. Certainly here I could find someone to match my Mr. Benson. I got a beer at the bar and looked around. Motorcycle cops and body-builders and almost every fantasy I had ever developed spread through the room, just for me to choose from!

My first mark was a man wearing more leather than the animal had original skins. A heavy black mustache and a ring through his left ear completed a picture of such harshness and crude force that I no longer cared about Mr. Benson's naturalness. There was something to kneel down to—I could have knelt down right there to drink his piss, right in the bar. I sucked down my beer, glared at his blunt face, saw a glance come my way from underneath the leather cap.

I went over beside him. Sweat, welcome tension, came from my underarms as I thought about the loft I was sure he would live in. There would be chains suspended from exposed beams. I saw spotlights focused on my own flesh, naked and open to his he-man grasp.

"Girlfriend! What are you doing here? And in full leather drag!"

I was stunned when another fully dressed leather man came up to my prey and started to talk. Shop talk, and shop was the stock market. And then they talked about their children. Children? That had me thrown for a loop until I suddenly realized that their children were pedigreed dogs. I shoved through the crowd, desperate to leave before I found out that their dogs were poodles.

I went into the dark back. Not a real "backroom" but a place where a group of hunky-looking men could stand around and stare at one another while watching the line curving toward the urinals. I got my attitude together and went over to the center of the room. I spread my legs and watched the line of pissers. Started to seek their crotches. I got hard thinking about their golden fluids flowing out into the bowls. Thinking about licking, drinking, sucking. My cock could respond to these men. I didn't need Mr. Benson and his overwhelming self-assurance. No, I looked at the one in a black undershirt slouched against the wall, pushing against the surface as he waited his turn.

The Ramrod was no place to drink piss. This wasn't a backroom, but the basket on that number! I glared at his middle. I was so intent on that midsection that I was shocked when I looked up and saw him staring back at me. Hot man. Here's one I could get it on with real good. I opened my mouth to show

43

interest when suddenly it dawned on me. I had to stop for a minute and think. It couldn't be, but it was. There on his right side hung a set of heavy keys, and in the back right pocket a bright yellow handkerchief. He was another bottom.

By now I was dejected. Weren't there any men left in New York City?

I could try one more beer and see what else came in. I could, and I could end up doing that for every night this year. I was not going to meet Mr. Benson on Sunday afternoon at the Ramrod. I never have figured out why he had been in the other bar in the first place. Why had I happened to run into him that one night? But it dawned on me that it would be many nights before I ever met him in a bar again. If I ever met him in a bar again.

I sadly put down my bottle and wove my way through the crowd. Decisions had been made. It was time to put it on the line. My own inclinations that afternoon had been right. I would have to call Mr. Benson and tell him that now I knew that the only way for me to go on was to do it as his one and only.

Mr. Benson would be my real master, not a fantasy for the night.

THREE

Of course, I had been to the Mineshaft before, but only once or twice. This was the heaviest leather bar in New York, the source of half the gossip of my circle of acquaintances. "You know what *he* did at the Mineshaft last night?" That was the normal prelude to a bar dish among the fluff queens. Tonight, I walked with a purpose up the stairs to the second floor entrance to be tested by Mr. Benson.

A week had dragged by since last I had seen him. I called Monday to tell him my decision about the future. I told him clearly, even calmly, that I was offering myself as his slave, that I wanted to take the test he had prescribed to see if I could be good enough, obedient enough, sexy enough to pass his inspection. His response was hard and pointed. He had spent plenty of time setting his standards. There were things which Mr. Benson would not tolerate.

One of them was my job. He explained carefully that he had no intention of dealing with someone running off to clerk at an insurance company when there were things to be done in the house. He gave me an option that I accepted. I wouldn't need the job if I went to live with him; I would have to trust him to provide for me. He suggested that I take a week's vacation. If I went to live with Mr. Benson, it wouldn't matter if I returned, but the week would be a kind of second test. If I failed, I could leave his house and go back to my 9–5 ritual of humiliation-for-pay.

I would also have to give up the apartment and my few goodies from Bloomies. Mr. Benson thought I had little worth carting around.

So, I would have two tests: this Saturday night and then a whole week, after which I would have to decide again if I was ready to make a commitment so intense that it would leave no room for my friends and furniture.

The week of fantasy leading up to the climbing of these stairs bounced me through many conflicting thoughts about my trial. I looked forward to it sexually. I wanted to taste the piss flowing through Mr. Benson's long, sensuous cock, I wanted to lick his good-tasting pit sweat, I wanted to feel his fist glide up my ass again. But there was also fear. That one previous night had been the heaviest SM trip I had ever endured. What if I couldn't take any more? What if I had only gone through it because of a passing fancy for that handsome man? What if the pain overtook the pleasure and I lost it?

Doubts started through my mind as I handed the Mineshaft bouncer the entrance fee and saw him look over my clothes. He was not impressed with my Adidas sneakers, but to some they are a fetish. The rest, well, he didn't know about the rest. I eased past him into the first room, the bar of the Mineshaft. The early crowd had begun to line the walls of the room. Leather, denim, and skin alternated in the rows of bodies out for early display. I had my orders. I went to the coat check and began my obedience number, just as Mr. Benson had ordered me.

The coat check at the Mineshaft is different from any other bar's in New York. They don't limit themselves to customers' jackets. The man behind the counter hardly blinked as I stripped off my jacket, then my pants, my shirt and, finally, even my sneakers.

I think that the sneakers were the part that had bothered me the most. The Mineshaft was not a place where I wanted my bare feet to make contact with the floor. But the orders had been explicit: at midnight I was to be standing in front of the fake wooden rail fence in the front bar, and I was to be wearing only a jockstrap.

Waiting for Mr. Benson.

The jockstrap didn't produce a second glance in a place so used to them; a sign on the wall said that the Jockstrap League of America met here once a month. A couple cowboys admired what they called my "flat golden nipples." An "Indian" liked my body with its rounded pecs. One particularly mean-looking state trooper started to come over, but a subtle shaking of my head staved him off. I leaned back against the fence and watched the game being played on the pool table. It was not pool.

The clock over the bar said that I had fifteen minutes to countdown. I debated a beer. I had been smart enough to put a couple bucks in my pouch. I was dry-mouthed with tension, waiting for a climax to a week of solitude with my thoughts, fears, and fantasies. I went over and got a Bud, ignoring the comments and the looks as I leaned my bare ass over the counter to place my order. I took the good-tasting suds back over to the fence and put a foot up on the first rung.

Waiting for Mr. Benson.

I kept wondering what form the test would take.

Why the Mineshaft? There was only one answer to that question; Mr. Benson intended to make this a public event. I had realized that from the beginning. My stomach felt light as I thought about all these eyes watching me now, and what they would see after Mr. Benson arrived. I remembered my body sprawled on his floor, sucking his toes, licking his feet, his instep crushing down on my open jaws. Would I be doing that here tonight? With his boots? Would I be polishing them with my tongue while he lashed at me with a belt? A riding crop? A whip?

I remembered the piss-drinking, its golden flow down my throat. Would Mr. Benson repeat that here in the Mineshaft? Right in the front room? With all these people watching me gulp down his manwater?

I remembered the other deeper and darker rooms in the joint. Through that corridor was the room with the sling. A black leather sheath suspended from the ceiling. I had seen men climb up and in and open their asses to some stud standing greasy-fisted in front of them, widening the groove of their pain-fucking cheeks, forcing their limbs into the body. Was Mr. Benson going to do that to me in front of all these men? Would he let them pinch and tug at my tits while he worked his fist in and out of my butt? Would he make me suck their alien cocks?

Beyond that was a dark room, the least lit in the place, where the game was cocksucking. Was Mr. Benson going to take me in there? Would I end up spending the whole evening licking these men's pricks, drinking their come? Giving them all the pleasure they wanted?

And downstairs there was another dark room with walls slippery with ooze. Was Mr. Benson going to take me downstairs into that room and add my screams of pain to all the echoes of past beatings that had taken place there? Would they all gather around and watch him cut my backside with deep lashes from a coiled leather snake?

The second room had a bathtub in the center. Was Mr. Benson going to put me in it? Was he going to let all the anonymous bodies piss on me? Would he make me drink their gallons of urine? Would he pull me out of the place soaked, my hair carrying the stench of aggressive men?

Or the last room—another bar—would Mr. Benson drag me into the dim light on the stage in that last room? Would he auction me off to the highest bidder? Or the biggest cock? Force me to do whatever man, god or troll, climbed up on the stage with me? The pouch of my jock strained against my pulsing dick as I catalogued the possible adventures.

I should have known that Mr. Benson would have done none of them. After five years I know now that Mr. Benson is too much of an elitist to let me be used and abused by just anyone. Then there are his friends, and I was about to learn how much Mr. Benson values friendship.

The crowd at the Mineshaft must be the most jaded in New York. There is almost nothing that they haven't seen take place right there in those six rooms and the two toilets. Every trip from rubber to wingtip shoes had been celebrated in its walls, but still there was a sudden hush when The Presence came into the room. I hadn't been paying attention. I was too far gone in the fantasies of my evening to see It coming, but I heard the silence. I looked up and saw him standing there, directly in front of me.

The black doorman from that first night.

He was wearing a very different type of uniform now than last week. He had on a black motorcycle cap. A tan uniform shirt with a black belt stretched across his chest. Then black leather britches, shiny with care, and exaggerated by a strip of white leather down each thigh.

I don't know if I had appreciated his immensity before. His body towered over me, even taller than Mr. Benson's, but he had none of Mr. Benson's sleek lines, only menacing bulk in front of my face.

"Are you ready for Mr. Benson, boy?"

I was speechless except for a nod: *Yes!*

He reached up and attached a dog collar to my neck; its stiff leather felt comfortably uncomfortable from the start. Then he reached into his pockets and took out handcuffs. He joined my wrists behind my back. Then he pulled sharply on the leash and led me out down the stairs and into the waiting car. He just led me, naked and barefoot into the New York winter night.

No one in the bar dared say anything. They correctly assumed that I went willingly. And I was willing, but scared shitless. He shoved me onto the floor of the back seat of the new Mercedes, locked the door, strode to the front, and folded his bulk into the driver's seat. We sped off through the Village streets. It only took a few minutes actually, until he stopped and dragged my shivering body out into the middle of a warehouse district I couldn't recognize. South of Canal Street? North of Chelsea? Who knew?

He led me into one of the warehouse buildings through a door marked only with the smallest of signs: THE TOPMEN.

I was suddenly right under a light bulb. The black man announced my arrival. "Mr. Benson, your new pet."

As I gratefully warmed up in the well-heated room and adjusted my eyes to the third-degree glare, I found seven men lounging around on old furniture, all holding beer cans, all dressed in the same black-and-tan leather outfits as my captor.

The best of them was Mr. Benson.

I was going to see the interior of this room often; I would end up here in Mr. Benson's clubhouse many more nights than I could have predicted. This was where Mr. Benson liked to pass his rare social hours. There are seldom guests in the penthouse, and I had been correct when I had assumed that Mr. Benson and the other Topmen liked to spend their time together here in this ancient warehouse, far from the ears and cares of intruding, curious people.

Mr. Benson actually smiled as I looked at him across the room. I used to mistake actions like smiles from Mr. Benson to be things like welcomes. That was no welcome. Tom, the doorman, had unthinkingly begun a new game.

Mr. Benson played it out. He strode over to me and put a hand on my neck; turning to the other Topmen, he said, "A pet, gentlemen. My new pet."

They laughed uproariously.

"I had thought to introduce you to my new slave, but I think Tom is right. It's more accurate to think of this fine specimen of *humanus sclavus* as a pet: one who, I am sure, will bring me many hours of pleasure and companionship."

His little speech was delivered with a great dramatic flair. The audience responded appropriately by applauding the presentation.

"Mr. Benson," one called out over the applause. "What *kind* of pet is this?"

I looked up at the speaker, easily the most handsome of the group: blond, blue-eyed, clean-shaven with a squared frame that provided a fully muscled body. Yet the swastika on his armband gave rise to the greatest reaction of fear.

51

"A pig, Benson, that's what he is, a pig!" The second one to contribute piped in; he was just as easily the least attractive. His Hindenburg body bulged incredulously against the smart uniform that added to the others' military-sharp appearance.

"In that case, Porytko, he certainly would be willing to suck even your cock." Mr. Benson tugged hard on my leash and pulled me over to stand in front of the overweight giant. As I came closer, I realized that he wasn't really ugly. He had a different look, a Slavic bluntness that became macho good-looking when it was more closely inspected. I was learning that masculine beauty was lots more than Hollywood Handsome. His bulk was also deceptive; his size had led me to think him fat, but the force was with him as he worked his arms to pull his fat uncut cock out of his pants. Mr. Benson leaned down on my neck as the gargantuan Polack started his baiting call, "Come on, sooee, come on, little piggy, show us how much you can eat." The crowd picked up his taunts. I went to my knees and took the fat Polish sausage, its girth stretching the corners of my throat and its fleshy length striking the back of my mouth. The stranger pulled on my ears and shoved his whole Slavic prick into me, forcing me to gag with almost every stroke. My only recourse was to open up as willingly as I could. After only a minute of ramming himself down my helpless body, he shot a thick load of salty come down my gullet. Intense. In record time.

"Now, Porytko, who's the pig?" Mr. Benson exclaimed. He watched me gulping down the hot ooze.

"Mr. Benson!" A squatly built bearded man, sitting next to the Pole, said: "I think the pig looks more like a cat, myself."

"Yeah, a cat!" The men toyed with me. With a

heightening intensity, Mr. Benson asked the group, "And what is going to prove him a cat?"

"Well, Mr. Benson, I know that mine has a tongue that won't stop going. Licks me everywhere."

Mr. Benson jerked my neck up off the Polish cock, the sharp tug on the stiff collar forcing my face to look up into his. "Well, asshole, why aren't you licking me?" The humor left his face. He spit full down upon me, the viscous fluid splattering over my nose and cheeks. "You don't like me as much as Mark's cat likes him?"

I was terrified by this new game. There was none of the quiet masterfulness I had seen in Mr. Benson before. None of the underflow of caring strength that had attracted me in the beginning. This was pure cruelty, I thought. These men, their uniforms, ganging up on me. But the fear made me rub my face directly in Mr. Benson's crotch and start to lick at the bulge I knew was there. I wasn't going to fail! Neither him nor me!

"Mr. Benson." I couldn't see which one was speaking now. "My cat does more than lick; the poor thing's forever drinking out of a toilet bowl!" That raised every man's high spirits. Mr. Benson played off the perfect new cue. He got me up onto my feet. My hands bound behind me threw me off balance as I struggled to keep up with the figure moving through applause to a doorway across the room.

Luckily, the doorman's body broke my fall and his strong arm helped me on the way as I went into the bathroom behind Mr. Benson. I was surprised when the lights went on and I saw how large it was—much too large for the clubhouse; it had two urinals and two toilets. The walls and floors were immaculate white-and-black tile, freshly scrubbed. I was to see a lot more of this room in the future. The care they had put into it should have prepared me. One good toilet deserves another. It takes one to know one.

I hadn't seen the signal Mr. Benson must have given the doorman, who unlocked my handcuffs. The group had followed us into the large room and was forming a semicircle. "Hey, Mr. Benson, wait a minute." The Pole spoke out as he stepped up to the toilet in front of where we were standing. He smiled broadly as he pulled out his dripping dick and immediately started to piss in the bowl. Thick yellow streams flowed into the clear water. It was all too apparent to me what was happening. I took a deep breath just as the hands behind me forced me down on my hands and knees and pushed my head toward the white porcelain.

My face entered the cold water while the chunk of a man above me was still pissing his bladder out. He soaked my hair; piss ran down the sides of my face and into my mouth. They ordered me from above to slurp up the toilet water.

The others, or at least some of them, joined in and within seconds, streams of hot piss flowed down my back into the bowl. The different shades of their piss were mixing into the toilet bowl. It was my bowl now! I was not going to fail so early! I was going to show them. I was going to show Mr. Benson. I not only drank the water, I drank it eagerly. Two weeks before I would have fainted at the thought of the stinking fluids, but now I sought them out. My tongue lapped the different streams down the white surface. I slurped noisily.

As the whole ordeal kept going, the pride in me matched my defiance. I was not going to let them win over me so easily. I was going to prove myself to Mr. Benson. I would find manly nobility at the bottom.

When he finally pulled up on the leash, I was

bloated. The stink of all the men filled my nose. The slurping had left trails of water and piss streaking down my chest, drenching my elastic jockstrap.

There was a quieter sense to the laughter as they put their cocks back into the uniform pants. A cat? Okay, a cat! I remembered the first story and went back with my mouth to Mr. Benson's crotch, pulling my tongue over the slick leather of his uniform, burying my nose in the full curve of his flesh. His hand petted the back of my head.

"Hey, Mr. Benson!"

"Now, what?" Mr. Benson was less raucous as he continued to pet me.

"Well, Mr. Benson, since this is sort of a universal kind of pet, why don't you show him? You know, like at those Madison Square Garden fancy dog shows?"

Laughter.

Without further words, Mr. Benson pulled up on the leash and led me back into the first room. The doorman pulled out a stand; it was the size of a small dining room table. "Up, boy!" Mr. Benson slammed his fist on its surface.

I climbed on and knelt up on my knees. Mr. Benson came to the side of the table as the group returned to their seats in obvious anticipation of this next primal act. Mr. Benson picked up some of his showmanship again. "Gentlemen, this fine specimen is a blue-ribbon without doubt." He reached over and ran a hard hand down my side, emphasizing each point in his monologue. "Notice the smooth lines, the full chest, slimming into a tight waist, and filling out again into fine, rounded hips." Whistles greeted his hand's progress around to my ass.

"Yeah, but, Mr. Benson!" It was the sturdy dark man again. "When you have an animal that has lines as fine as those, well, you should be doing something to bring them out. You know, they shouldn't be covered with all that unnatural cloth."

Mr. Benson agreed and jerked down my jock to expose my half–hard-on and my balls, pulled up with fear and excitement. There was low moan of approval. Mr. Benson put up his hand to calm their dripping lust. "Now, of course, our good brother here is correct, there should be nothing to interfere with such obviously championship qualities."

"But, Mr. Benson, he has hair!"

"Never fear! You should certainly know that hair never lasts long in my household." New laughter clued me that the last's remark was a bow to Mr. Benson's own special tastes. Obviously this was the opening for something Mr. Benson had planned all along. The black doorman brought over a simple bag, a doctor's black house-call case. Mr. Benson opened it on the table and placed a can of shaving cream, a deadly straight-edged razor and a long, wide razor strop on the top. Accompanied by the appreciative noises of his audience, he went over to a nearby wall and attached the strop to a ring screwed directly into the brick. With his most dramatic gesture yet, he sharpened the straight edge with long graceful strokes. For my pleasure? The group's? Or his own?

The appearance I was putting in on the table was almost a relief. Whether it was the sudden realization that this had more in common with a fraternity hazing than anything else, or whether it was the sudden surge of pride and resolve on my part, or whether it was the sudden pride in Mr. Benson's compliments on my body, I'm not sure. It may also have been the fascination with which I watched him sharpen the instrument on the strop. I couldn't help but anticipate what was coming. I certainly knew that my crotch fur was going to go. Was any more? I looked down on my chest and saw the few strands of hair that had been so proudly growing across to join my nipples. Before that moment, I don't think that I had ever really thought much of the hair under my armpits. Would that sweaty mat be sheared too?

Mr. Benson came back over. The room was quieter now as the men sat back to savor this next act of the show. My cock started to fill. They didn't laugh at its growing hardness; they chuckled knowingly. A cool handful of stiff suds was rubbed over my cock and balls. Then in the clump of hair over them. The wave of foam went up to my navel. Expertly, smoothly, Mr. Benson touched the cold steel to the base of my cock and scraped up, taking with the metal edge almost all of my brown bush. He repeated the long strokes with slow, deliberate care until my crotch was almost totally stripped of any covering.

Then he grabbed my now fully-hard prick and moved around to stand almost directly in front of me, pulling the sharpened edge down the length of my tool. Then he grasped my balls and stretched them to their limit; the steel cleaned off my double sac in shorter strokes. I was breathless as Mr. Benson peeled the covering from the delicate egg shapes. I dared take gulps of air only in between the runs of his steel on my flesh.

He stood aside when he had finished and wiped the blade almost carelessly on my flanks. A soft whistle came from the men in front of me as they looked over my totally sheared flesh.

"But, now…" Mr. Benson smiled as he put down the antique shaver. He manipulated my body until I had turned away from the audience and then forced my head down on the wooden surface, leaving my ass sticking in the air. He pulled my legs apart at the knees, exposing my asshole to the group. I felt the foam being applied again, its sudden chill going up and down my crack. I clenched my fists as I prepared for the rasping metal against my delicate hole. At first I had my eyes closed, waiting. When I felt the steel hardness against my thin-skinned vulnerability, I pulled up on my butthole.

It was then that I saw it. In front of me, now that I had my face away from the table. Standing over in the corner of the room where I couldn't have noticed it before. I hardly paid any attention to the rest of the shaving. I barely heard the comments on the excellence of the job being done by Mr. Benson. The new sight gripped me with fear. Could I withstand that? Would I be able to take it? I should have known that I would have no choice.

I have never found out if Mr. Benson or the others had noticed my noticing, or whether it was really planned that they would grab me. From beyond my sight, their hands reached out and took hold of my ankles and then my wrists. They pulled without questions; they stretched my body against the table, my waist cutting into its edge. Two of them must have sat on the floor in order to maintain the pressure on my legs. Two others I could see as they held my arms sharply against the corners of the top.

I could see Mr. Benson as he came back around the table, this time walking past me and over to the corner where he bent down to pick up the handle that rested over the edge of the brazier, its wooden end protected from the hot coals that had turned the metal edge red with heat.

There was no circus hint in Mr. Benson's voice now. "Men, this slave is mine. He's come here of his own free will. He's agreed to be in my service. These games have been fun, but it's time we got down to the business of establishing ownership." He had walked around to the back of me. Cold sweat ran down my forehead. My guts wrenched. I turned my face over and opened my mouth to bite my arm. I would not scream.

Mr. Benson held the branding iron for all to see.

Then he lowered it below and behind my line of sight. My butt sizzled. I smelled my body cooking, like so much meat. Tears streamed out of my eyes. A sigh of appreciation came from the men around me. I thought that I would faint from the rush of pain that tore through me, reaching out from my right buttock, now, forever, marked by Mr. Benson. They let go of me almost as soon as the act was over. I was so shocked with the glowing hurt, I stood there, bent over the table, grasping its edge even after they had released me.

A cool hand went over my ass, smoothing a salve of some kind, but shocking my skin over the wound. The sudden new wave of sensation jerked me upright. The black doorman was beside me, the strange medicine sending its smell into my nose. The sobs still heaved in my chest from my cries. I tried to hold them back, to regain myself. "Come here, boy. You aren't finished yet."

I closed my eyes in a sense close to desperation.

What more?

What more could he want?

The fire burned in my shanks as I faced him.

There it was. The Source. Mr. Benson's hard cock hung out, celebrating my pain and marking. His heavy balls hung down over the snaps of his leather codpiece. I went over to him, wincing at every movement of my butt, dragging my right leg to try to keep it stiff, but giving up when I reached him and swallowing to ready myself for the quick rage of pain as I knelt and prayerfully took his beautiful cock in my mouth.

I knelt in communion with Mr. Benson like a religious fanatic who had journeyed to a shrine. My week of abstinence, my humiliation, my trial, had all been for this. This godstick and these ripe and full nuts hanging beneath my chin. I went mad with desire for his cock. Oblivious to my branded butt, I chowed down on the pole in front of me.

Mr. Benson's cock.

His fabled virility poked down my throat. I worked my head and neck to feel his smooth surface against my inside. Before long, his shaft began to swell with come. The veins pushed against the outer layer of skin. I gulped further down at the early warning and, when he shot, the precious juice pistoled straight into me, hardly any of it even into my mouth, the taste of this man—I can say it now—went straight to my soul!

Five years ago all that happened.

I have never been allowed to grow back my man-hair. The scar on my buttock, of course, has cured to a fine mark. But now the sensation of that seems so far away that I think it more pride than pain because it is Mr. Benson's mark on me: a large B in a simple circle.

The night, that first night, was not over. But the branding brought a climax to my center-stage performance. Tom took me over to the doorway of the toilet when Mr. Benson's cock was finished with me. The enormous black reapplied my handcuffs and pushed me back down on my knees, reawakening the pain in my buttocks. The last joke of the evening came from Porytko, who put a roughly lettered sign around my neck: TOILET. The Topmen went back to their drinking and smoking, ignoring me for a while except when they took the sign literally.

I drank more piss that night than I had imagined

doing in my fantasies at the Mineshaft. The sharp taste burned in my mouth, relieved only by each new load that one of the club members brought over to me as the great amounts of beer flushed out his system. Twice my own water flowed unnoticed on the floor. It was the first time that I was able to watch these men as a group; I listened to them talk, trying to figure out who was who and what was going on, and trying to forget the brand that still sent shock waves through my body every time I moved.

Tom, the black doorman, was obviously an attendant to Mr. Benson. Some sort of second lieutenant. There is no doubt from the way he acted that his presence was because of my new master. His huge size and the terror he would throw in the eyes of anyone who saw his thickly sculptured African face was betrayed by the care he gave Mr. Benson's needs, and even mine. Tom was, after all, the man who applied the salve to my wound that night.

If Tom was a stereotype in any way, the other black in the group was the opposite. From the conversation, even through my pain, I could tell that Brendan was a cop. I was startled by the thought of his tall stature in a deep blue uniform and was able to spend a lot of time wondering if it would look any better buttoned and zipped and strapped into the outfit of New York's finest than it did in the Topmen's uniform.

Brendan talked with a drawl that was almost Southern; probably at some point it was, but its edge was cut with an academic ability that showed itself whenever he and Mr. Benson talked. They were obviously the most intelligent of the group, and they enjoyed that intelligence greatly. Often, it would seem that they would have to check their conversation or risk leaving the others, more brawn than brains, behind.

More often, Porytko would stop them before they had a chance to get too far. They never seemed to mind the good-natured hulk breaking in with a joke that too often seemed funny only to him. The big guy's deep laugh would fill the room often with self-congratulatory guffaws. He was easily the least sinister of the group. But he could spit a hawker over twenty feet right on the target!

The most sinister, by far, was the German they called Hans. The others used my mouth to piss in so casually that they seemed to just want to save themselves the walk into the toilet behind me. But when Hans came over, he would reach down and take my tits between his fingernails. His vise-grip squeeze-tortured my smooth brown nipples. My gasps of pain he muffled with the heavy uncut cock he shoved in my mouth. Once Mr. Benson stopped him with a sharp call when he was reaching down to scratch at my fresh brand. I had to psych myself every time that Hans stood to approach me and get my tender nipples ready for the sharp action he sadistically loved to give them.

Mark, the man who had talked about the cat, was the most self-conscious of all, I thought. His attitude seemed a little too studied as he pulled up his belt every time he approached me. His scowl seemed more put-on than the natural curl of the lip that Hans showed. He seemed to have the least to say to the rest of the group. He seemed to want almost to change places with me.

The two most talkative, really, and the two most unlikely—and the two who would have driven my old bar friends crazy with lust—turned out to be lovers. They were two matched Italians, both well over six feet tall, both heavy-chested, hair pouring up over their collars, both rich with sweet-smelling piss and tasty cocks. Their dark black mustaches were full and regulation-clipped on their olive faces. The completion of the fantasy for all to acknowledge came when they talked of the construction company they jointly owned, and the weights they jointly worked out with. Frank and Sal were strange partners; their demeanor was so obviously masculine and their conversation with the other men regarding sex showed they were both masters, but their manly affection for one another was somehow a natural part of their being between them.

The Topmen.

They were all in that group. I'd learn later that there were bottoms that they owned. Some, though, like Mark, were loners, or like Hans, could never have expected anyone to stay around that long. Frank and Sal had little room left in their relationship for a third person to stay. Only Mr. Benson and Brendan had the strength to rule any one person as fully as Mr. Benson would rule me for the next five years.

The beer and the smoke got to them. My exhausted body lay over in the corner, but the agonies I had endured must have turned them on. The evening was drawing to a close as I watched an early morning light come in over the crack in the doorway; the Topmen would come in and take their pleasure—all except, thankfully, Hans.

Brendan the cop was the biggest. I was shocked when his huge tool had first been pulled out to piss up my ass. And I was delighted to take on the task of trying to accommodate the member when he brought it again swollen with lust over to me. This time I chewed on his long, black foreskin as it passed through my teeth that first time. He loved it. I had marveled at the pinkness of the front of his prick when I had first seen it peek out from under the folds; the contrast was sharp against the dark shaft-skin.

The sexiest, most tender encounter was when Frank and Sal came over together and used my face as a hole to fuck while they made out over me. Their sloppy kisses and hard "Do it, man" slaps left me with a raging hard-on after first one, then the other, had shot into me.

Mark strode over and drove into my mouth. He like to talk dirty. His monologue describing my piss-drenched and come-saturated body seemed more for his own turn-on than for my debasement.

Tom came over almost perfunctorily. He was laughing as he stuck his stick in my bruised and bleeding mouth.

Hans glowered from where he sat. Was he angry that Mr. Benson had stopped him from inflicting too much pain on me? Had Mr. Benson stopped him from going over this last time to join everyone else in climaxing the evening? Whatever, he left abruptly, saying he was off to the Mineshaft to see if there was anyone worthwhile left for him.

The others took this as their cue and got up to leave. They departed one by one leaving the mess of beer cans and filled ashtrays. I remember I used to wonder who had the job of cleaning up. I wondered who had ever assembled this extraordinary group of Manhattan men. But the thoughts didn't go far. As soon as they had left me alone and the continual flow of piss and come into me ceased, I had given in to a burden of fatigue and slumped down, the only thing even slowing my sliding into immediate sleep being the pain as my raw wound hit the floor. But I did sleep. Or pass out.

I didn't wake until we were standing in the elevator of Mr. Benson's apartment. I wasn't standing. I was in Tom's arms. The two faces smiled down at me, ignoring my stench.

Even with the draperies nearly closed, the sun streaked into Mr. Benson's apartment. I had no sense of time left. Only a relief to be at home.

Home!

A sudden start! I understood for the first time that, after only one night, this was home.

With the least possible aid from me, Tom lowered me into a warm and soothing bath. He dried my weak body and put on more of his strange salve, covering it with a gauze bandage. The collar had left my neck stiff, the skin red from its rubbing. I chafed my wrists, which showed deep red gashes where the steel handcuffs had bruised me to the bone.

Mr. Benson played for real.

When my nude, nearly hairless body was dried, Tom took me into the living room. Mr. Benson was waiting. He had drunk and smoked noticeably less than the rest of the group. Now he sat in his favorite chair, stripped down to his leather britches, sipping out of an amber glass. He smiled a welcome to the two of us. Tom deposited me and went wordlessly on his way. I sank onto the floor, sprawling once again at his feet, desperately tired and hoping he wouldn't want more from me now.

"Well, boy, that wasn't really a test. I was sure you had firmly made up your mind." He paused while he sipped. "We'll consider it a beginning to your training."

"Yes, Sir." I could barely get the words out.

Then Mr. Benson, the tyrant of this night of nights, reached down and gathered my body into his arms. I wrapped one of my own arms around his shoulders and put my head against his chest.

65

"Boy."

I looked up.

Mr. Benson bent his neck down and softly, but firmly, kissed my bruised lips. That was all I remembered that night. When I woke up in my sleeping bag the next morning, I could only hope that his affection would be repeated.

Tough and tender, the kiss from Mr. Benson made me feel proud to be a man so valued by another man.

FOUR

The next time I woke up, Mr. Benson was standing beside me. He had one of his noncommittal looks on his face. Not really warm, certainly not cold, it was a look that kept you guessing and wondering what was going on inside his head. He was dressed in jeans, a white T-shirt and heavy engineer boots. His freshly shaven face was covered by shadows from the over-hanging light.

"Get up, asshole."

I jumped off the sleeping bag and up onto my knees. Sleep kept my eyes from opening comfortably. I couldn't adjust to the sudden glare.

"Kiss my boots." Sleepiness or no, I knew that tone of voice. This wasn't the time to plead a headache. Mr. Benson was obviously going to start off right away this morning. My head went down and my tired lips grazed the rough leather of the boots.

"The other one." I went over to the second heavy stomper and caressed it. I thought I was finished and started to sit up again.

Quickly, the long piece of leather in Mr. Benson's hand reached out and cut across my chest. "I didn't tell you to get up." I dove back down and tried to think about the sharp surface of the leather, not about the red line of pain streaked across my body. Finally, he told me to get on my knees.

The waking-up ritual was something I hadn't expected. My mind was foggy with sleep. Only that strip of pain joining my nipples made me know this wasn't a nightmare.

Mr. Benson held out the leather. It was a riding crop. I had only seen them before in movies. Its hard stem was tipped with a menacing loop of animal skin.

"Kiss this." My trembling lips reached across and touched that frightening appendage. "This is going to be one of your best friends for the next few weeks. He's going to be your teacher. You're going to learn to obey him." Now I understood the reasons for all this. After the initiations at the clubhouse last night, I was about to start my real training.

I never once saw Mr. Benson without that crop for the next month. I learned to anticipate its stinging touch. "Every morning you start in, right away. The first thing you do when you see your master is kiss his feet—bare, booted, whatever. And you stay there until your master gives you permission to get up. Do you understand?" The loop of the crop reached down and circled one of my tits.

"Yes, Sir."

"Go make me a cup of coffee. Hurry up." The loop flicked out at my nipple and made me bound right off the floor and into the kitchen.

Mr. Benson was sitting, reading his newspaper, when I placed the cup of hot liquid beside him. "Go take a shower, but don't use my bathroom. Use the one in the maid's room off the kitchen. When you're finished, just stay there. Don't dry yourself off."

This whole thing was becoming ominous. Why was Mr. Benson being so hard and cold? And what was

going to happen that I couldn't even dry myself off? I
did go, of course, even as scared as I was. And under
the warm flow of the shower I thought about my
pledges to him. My promise to try to be a good slave.
I was finally waking up and my awareness was making me remember my resolutions. I finished and
stood waiting for Mr. Benson with the water dripping
down my body.

I had begun to shiver by the time he came into the
room.

"Turn around." He wanted to see my brand. I had
removed the bandage to shower. The scab had at
least formed and, even though there were dull aching
pains every time I moved, I was very proud of it.
Very proud to have Mr. Benson's mark on my body.
The frightening crop made a circle around the mark,
but thankfully never touched it.

"Every morning, when I'm here or when you're
alone, the next thing you do is shave your body. It is a
task you should learn to do reverently. It is the ritual
of preparing yourself for me…"

He took a mirror down off the wall and put it on
the seat of the toilet. "Lift up your leg and you'll be
able to watch yourself."

He handed me a razor and a can of shaving cream
and kept guard as I lathered my still-damp body with
suds. The slick feeling of the soap on my crotch
caused my cock to swell. The skin around my ass had
no hair on it after the night's shaving, and it slid
against my lubricated hand. The whole action was
erotic in a new sense for me. I took the razor and
started to scrape the hard metal against the bristle of
my crotch hair. Then I pulled out the sac holding my
balls and cut away the soap, leaving the skin pink
with sensation. The hard part was to shave around
the puckered hole with just the reflection in the mir-

ror. Mr. Benson kept giving me words of encouragement and advice and, when I was finished, I think he and I were both proud of the extraordinarily nude result.

"That's good, boy, very good. It'll help you keep your mind in the right place at the start of each day. Now go clean up your sleeping area. We still have some things to talk about."

I went and rolled up the bag and put it back in its closet. Mr. Benson was sitting in the chair in the living room, waiting for my return, the leather stick still in his hands. "Kneel."

Once more I found myself looking up at him, aware of the hot bulge in front of my face. "Boy," he said, reaching beside himself and pulling out a small cardboard package, "this is clothing designed for a slave." He held up the package: a jockstrap! "Do you know why?"

I was honest and shook my head, admitting that I didn't know what he meant. "There's no reason for me to put up with the inconvenience of a slave's cock and balls. Sometimes they're alright to look at but most often they just get in the way. Now, a jockstrap keeps all the extraneous matter tucked away out of sight, but it still keeps the ass open, bare for a slap or a fuck. Whatever's best for the slave. You understand?" I nodded in agreement.

"Boy, I expect you to have a nice, clean, white jockstrap on all the waking time you spend in this apartment. There are some extras in the maid's room. You make sure you have one on every day after your shower. And you keep them clean."

He handed me the elastic pouch and straps. "Put it on." I stood and slipped on the tight cup. The pouch cupped my crotch, making me even more aware of it than I was when it was bare. The straps clung to the cheeks of my ass and outlined the nude crack between my mounds. It felt very good, and it made me feel very vulnerable.

"Turn around." I swiveled so my backside was to him. His hand came out and grabbed at one of my cheeks. "Your ass is one of the main reasons you're here, kid. Keep it clean and smooth and hard and you'll be around here for a long time." The hand lightly went over the scab of the brand. The muscle under it was sore, as though it were bruised, and even this lightest of touches from Mr. Benson made me start with renewed pain. "That's going to come out looking real good, boy."

"Yes, Sir." My response was surprisingly enthusiastic, even to me. I was getting turned on by this examination. My cock pressed out against the confining elastic of the jock. I was hoping this was all leading to sex. I was certainly ready for it.

"Go into my closet and get out the shoe polish kit. It's on the floor, right by the doorway." Disappointed, I went and retrieved the wooden box that was, of course, just where he said it would be. When I returned, he put out his foot. "Take care of my boots, boy." I got back down on my knees and took out the can marked black. I put the thick greasy polish over both his boots and then took out the heavy brush and started to work on the leather. He laid a boot on each one of my thighs. "A slave has to learn to take care of his master's things, boy. Every day you polish these boots, or whatever I have on. They should all shine. And each time you do it, you think about making your man look good." The loop of the crop came out and ran across the crown of my head, underlining all of his words with its light but threatening touch.

"I want you to think about those boots, boy, think about the feet inside them. Think about how much you want to lick the surface of the leather...how much you want to suck on the feet inside...Think about them rubbing into your mouth and pressing against your balls...Keep those boots in your mind, boy...You have to learn that every part of my body is to be taken care of, every part of my body is another chance for sex for you...I want you to get hard thinking about my toes...my fingers...every single part of my body."

The crop never stopped caressing my head, and my cock never stopped hardening. I was raging with the pressure from my erection as I worked on the boots, wiping at the surface with movements that became as loving as Mr. Benson's words. I took out the cloth in the kit to do the last shine on them. The gritty soles of the boots rubbed into my legs, and the pouch of the jock was lifted away from my surface by the engorged prick of mine.

Mr. Benson kept the crop rubbing against my forehead when I was finally finished. There was a smile on his face—he liked that erection. "Every day, boy."

Abruptly he stood. The crop slapped at my arm. "Come on, you're ready for the next lesson."

I followed him into his bathroom. "Kneel." I got down and watched as he took out the beautiful prick that kept me in a state of desire. I was hoping the exposed cock was for me, but he aimed it at the toilet bowl and I could only watch as he wasted a gorgeous flow of piss down into the porcelain. He tucked his cock away. This really was torture.

"Boy, a slave should regard everything about his master's body as something beautiful, something sexual. You like my piss, don't you?"

Did he ask the question or did the crop that was now playing with one of my tits? "Yes, Sir, I like your piss."

"Good. You'll get enough of it in the time to come. But right now I want you to concentrate on this toilet bowl. That's where I just pissed. It's where I shit. I spend time here, boy. A slave should think of a toilet bowl as his master's throne. Kiss the rim, boy."

I bent over and put my lips on the black surface of the seat. "That's where your master's bare ass goes, boy. Get some more feeling into it. Lick it." My tongue darted out and covered the whole round surface with spit as the fearsome riding crop started making moves on my bare ass again. "I bet you can smell what your master's ass would be like if it was open there on that bowl right now. I bet you can taste what his piss would be like if it was flowing out. Couldn't you, boy?"

I growled agreement. My cock was betraying me again, bursting against the jock, my mind full of memories of smells and sensations from Mr. Benson's body.

"Every morning, boy, you come in here and you clean out the bowl. Every single morning you make love to your master's throne. I want it shining whenever I come here. I want it glistening with the affection I expect you to show it."

It took me about five minutes to clean the outside surface, to get every bolt gleaming with the reflections of light. The betraying prick in my jockstrap wouldn't calm down. My mind was taking in everything Mr. Benson had said. I found myself actually thinking of the white porcelain as a throne; the tiled bathroom had become a royal reception hall to me. It was all something that had to be spotless in order to meet the requirements of this exalted personage, Mr. Benson.

"All right, boy. Those are the basics. The kiss, the

shave, the boots and the throne. Those are things I expect every day without fail. I never expect to have to remind you about them. Understand?"

"Yes, Sir."

"Now I have work to do. I want quiet." The crop began underlining his words with taps on my shoulder again. "Absolute quiet."

That became our ritual for the mornings. I learned those steps easily. Well, the learning was easy, and the execution wasn't any problem, but my prick was a real concern. The shaving every morning was the worst part. When I had to cover myself with warm, slippery foam, it was an immediate and painful erection. Once, only once, I tried to beat off. Mr. Benson caught me.

"What the fuck are you doing?" The crop lashed out and whipped my ass. I was caught completely off guard. I hadn't expected him to come in. I started to stammer an excuse, but I couldn't do it quickly enough to stop the motion as the leather slashed out again, this time hitting my arm. "Don't you know better than that? What if I wanted you?" The crop cut into my side.

"I'm sorry, Sir."

His eyes were alive with anger and fury. "You have to learn to live with needing me, boy. You can't be beating off every time you wake up. You only do that when I tell you. Understand?" The crop gave its most painful emphasis yet, right on my chest.

"Oh yes, Sir. I'm sorry, Sir." My eyes watered from the pain and fear of his anger. Everything I was was invested in this man. My life had become his. There could be only fear in the idea of his being angry with me.

And he got what he wanted; he always does. I was in a state of constant horniness with Mr. Benson. The small strip of clothing made me feel even more naked than I was. My shaving ritual and the rituals of taking care of his boots and throne meant that I started the day with a dedication to him and his body. I don't remember any time in those first few months that I didn't want him. I don't think my cock ever got to be really flaccid.

The morning rituals were wonderful. The afternoon rituals were easy. Mr. Benson worked at his desk or went out on business in the afternoon. I would quietly work in the kitchen or read in a corner of the room where I could get sunlight to warm my nakedness. Those were pleasant times. But when Mr. Benson was finished with his work, then the horrors began.

"Boy, your body's in good shape, but I want it better." He had bought a set of weights and some exercise equipment. Before dinner every night, he would take me into the refurbished maid's room and sit at a chair and watch me work out. There was a set of training exercises he had devised, and he had devised them in such a way that I could never, never have completed the required number.

"Your friend here," he would say, running his hand on the length of the riding crop, "is going to help you with your workouts." The number of sit-ups, for instance, was always moved up so I couldn't do the quota. The crop made up the difference. If I was three short, I would get three whacks with it: on my stomach for sit-ups, on my ass for push-ups, on my chest for pull-ups. That first month my body was never without bruises; my muscles ached constantly.

But even so, that wasn't the worst part. After the exercises, I would cook him a simple meal, usually steak or chops—and serve it to him. I quickly got to the point of trying to prolong that dinner for as much time as possible, trying to avoid the evening ritual.

"Those are your biggest weaknesses, boy." The loop of the crop had reached out and circled each of my tits that first time he explained it to me. "There's no excuse for a slave to have a set of flat tits. It's just not right. A slave's tits should be the easiest way for a master to control his boy. They should be so sensitive that they can give the greatest pleasure, and create the most pain, with the least work. Your little round nipples just won't do, boy."

Mr. Benson had devised a training experience for my tits, one that worked wonderfully for his purposes, and one that nearly broke me.

After dinner every night, he would take me into the living room. He would bring out leather handcuffs and attach them to my wrists. "Now, boy, don't you start whimpering even before we begin." But I would. Even as I would reach out my wrists for him, I would start to cry a little. He would attach another set of bands to my ankles and then take me to the wall of the apartment where there were barely noticeable hooks. They were spaced just so far away that when each of my limbs was attached to one of them, I was left spread out as far as possible.

Then Mr. Benson would go back and get clamps. "These are your friends, boy; they're going to make you a better slave, kiss them." I would have to purse my lips and rub my mouth against the cold steel. I would watch as one of Mr. Benson's warm hands would go down and grab one of my breasts. Then he'd take one of the clamps, serrated with sharp teeth, and spring it onto the tit. I never could control the first gasp when that happened. When each tit had a clamp biting into it, Mr. Benson would go to sit in his chair and watch.

In the beginning, I tried to beg him to release me.

It did no good. I should have known it wouldn't. But I cried out from the hot waves of pain that shot out of my nipples. He'd leave me there for an hour sometimes. My tits would bleed before they hardened up in scar tissue. Red rivulets would travel down my chest and over my stomach and stain my jockstrap. I would struggle uselessly against the restraints. The pain from those two little clamps tearing into my body every night was worse than anything else Mr. Benson did to me. For weeks, the small circles of flesh were so tender that Mr. Benson's slightest touch was more painful than the lashes of the riding crop.

He would watch me intently while I hung there. Every night I worked against the hooks and twisted my body, desperate to create any sensation I could that would take my mind off the metal eating into me. He loved that show. It was one of the times and one of the ways that I learned that Mr. Benson was a true sadist, not just a power person trying to control someone. His own lust would take over. When the sweat from my underarms was flowing down my sides, he would come over and smear it into my face, leaving me with the sour taste of myself. He would admire the tension of the muscles, running a hand over their surface. And worst of all was when he would lean down and take the metal-clasped tits into his mouth.

There was no room for my body to move as I screamed in agony. My chest filled with sobs as his tongue ran over the small exposed surface between the clamp's jaws.

It all turned him on. It turned him on something fierce. After each one of those sessions, Mr. Benson needed release. He would take me down off the hooks. "You look fucking good, boy." His erection would bulge out into my groin. I would collapse into his arms, the tension and the strain of the strange position having taken all the energy from me. He would usually do it right there on the floor. His need would rule out any more time being spent on building up to something. His cock would need me then. Not in five minutes, but immediately.

He would release the clamps, creating a sharp sensation, and then would take the sore, bruised nipples in his mouth, his teeth recreating the ridges where the clamps had bitten into me, his tongue moving against the scabbed surface, his mouth licking in the drops of blood where the skin had broken. He would usually just bring out his prick and lubricate it with only his spit. And he'd force his way quickly and painfully into my ass, ignoring my pleas for mercy.

"You're going to be a fucking good slave by the time I'm done with you, boy. You're going to learn to love it all. The boots…" His litany would begin, "the tits, the ass, everything about me, every part of me."

He would shoot deep inside of me more quickly than at any other time. His lust over my submission, my pain and his power combined to force the fastest orgasms he would ever have with me.

At first, when he had finished, I would have to take a long time to get up and go to my sleeping bag. I would hurt so badly that I had to hold even the soft surface of the bag away from my chest if I wanted to get any sleep.

But one night it changed. Something happened. I don't know how, or when or why. I guess my body just gave in. It had to. It couldn't take the punishments any more. It couldn't take the deep trauma of the waves of pain. The tits had developed a new covering. They had grown, as he wanted them to, into red, bright points standing straight out from my body. And suddenly one night there was no pain. My body just did not register pain. It was about halfway through a session against the wall. I took a deep breath and felt the sensation against my nipples; I could look down and see the newly grown protrusions. I was, for the first time, ready for him when he came over. The pain that had horrified me before had turned into my own lust. I don't think even Mr. Benson expected my response when he took the nipple into his mouth that night. The warmth of his tongue rubbing against me took my breath away in a whole new way. "Oh yes, Sir, that feels wonderful, Sir."

And it did. My mind had created pleasure from pain.

Sex that night, right there on the floor, was another new experience. I had become something, someone new through these exercises. My legs went up around his chest, inviting his invasion of my body. The sharp entry at my hole was met with a sudden thrust of my pelvis as my body arched to swallow his cock deep inside.

He pumped furiously at me in hunger and need and in pride. We both shot. I never had to touch my cock that night. I came from just the pulling of the elastic material over my bursting prick.

We were both spent afterwards. Mr. Benson was beside me on the floor. "Boy, you just may turn out to be the best slave I ever had." He smiled at me. I guess my smile back was strange. I was preoccupied. I had made a transition that frightened me with its intensity. But it had happened. I had to face it. Most of the things that had happened up to that point were things that I had suffered because of my need for Mr. Benson. This was different. I knew I had become a masochist.

From that point on, sensations were sensations to

me—simply and purely sensations. I could cross the boundary between pain and pleasure. And I owed it all to Mr. Benson.

I had the training down really well. Mr. Benson must have agreed, because he decided to let me be seen in public.

"Brendan is my best friend, boy. He and I are used to spending our Sunday afternoons together. We've taken a break from that routine since we each had a slave to break in. But it seems like the time is right for us to get back together again. He's coming over with his boy tomorrow.

"I want you to understand something. I believe that a slave is like anything else I own. My friends are welcome to it. If Brendan or any of the men ever tell you to do something, you do it. Understand?"

I nodded.

"And I expect you to show every one of my friends as much respect as you do me. That means you greet Brendan just as you would greet your own master.

"The other thing you might as well know now is that it's also all right for you to play with your fellow slaves. If you and Brendan's boy want to get into any games while he's visiting, that's okay. We'll all get along better if the two of you are friends."

Mr. Benson had been smiling as he told me the last part. I couldn't understand the humor in that. Sex with another slave? How could that happen? And why was Mr. Benson so pleased by the idea? I began to wonder if he had something up his sleeve.

I jumped and ran when the doorbell finally sounded. Brendan and his slave! I had fantasized a lot about this meeting. I had assumed that the slave would also be a black man. Wrong! When I threw the door open, there was the handsome, ebony figure in his New York police uniform, and behind him was Rocco, my friend the bartender.

My surprise didn't keep me from falling down and kissing the sharply polished surface of Brendan's uniform boots. It also didn't keep me from watching Rocco as he undressed. I assumed it was the ritual for visiting another master's house and that the same would be expected of me. When he was fully naked—No jockstrap! He must have had different rules than I did—he went over to Mr. Benson and fell to his hands and knees. When I saw those tattoos there was no doubt—this was Rocco, the one who had been tending bar the first night I had met Mr. Benson. Butch stud Rocco was Brendan's slave.

Brendan put an admiring hand on the brand on my ass. The scab had come off by then and left a vivid mark. "Looks good, Mr. Benson. You did a fine job." He patted my head next. "And got him trained as good as can be!"

Mr. Benson nodded to Rocco's kneeling figure. "You haven't done badly yourself, Brendan." And the two men smiled at one another, obviously very pleased with themselves. "Okay, boys, up."

We stood as the two men met in the center of the room and shook hands, starting a conversation and ignoring our presence. Rocco, who was totally naked, was blushing and had hung his head. I couldn't imagine what was going on, but I wanted to find out. I tried to catch his eye, but he wouldn't look up and just stood there avoiding me. Exasperated, I went to him, grabbed his arm and dragged him into the kitchen. When the swinging door had shut, I broke out with a loud whisper. "Rocco, we've got to be quiet. It's okay to be in here so long as we don't make any noise. So tell me, what happened? How did this happen to you? I didn't know you were a bottom! How long has this gone on?"

81

My questions came out rapid-fire. Rocco just stammered and finally said, "Jamie, I'm so embarrassed. I never thought you'd go through with it. I didn't know you'd be here."

"Rocco, that's not important. But yes, I went through with it. I've been here almost since that first night, but you...?"

"Can I have a beer?" I went to the fridge and got out two cans. Rocco went to sit at the kitchen table. I stopped him just in time. "We can't use furniture, even here. Come over to the pillows." Mr. Benson had let me put some oversized pillows on the floor for when I watched TV. Rocco followed me over. I couldn't wait for his story.

"I met Brendan over a year ago. I'd been seeing him off and on till last month when I finally gave in."

"Gave in to what?" My enthusiasm broke in.

"Jamie, well, he's a hard man. He believes in all this master and slave shit, especially between whites and blacks. He, well, he wanted me to be his slave. When I used to resist, he would keep on leaving me. Every time that happened and every time I went back to him—I had to go back, Jamie; he's the best man I've ever met—well, every time my punishment would get worse. I finally had to decide whether or not I wanted him. If I did, it meant following his rules and living life his way. Once when I left him, he wouldn't take me back until I agreed to let him whip me. Another time he made me pierce my tits." Rocco cupped his left chest to show me the hole through the nipple. "And every time I left, he refused to sleep with me and he would stop other men I wanted from sleeping with me. I have this thing for black men, Jamie, and, well, Brendan would either follow me around in his police uniform and scare them all away, or he'd tell them I was a racist, or he'd tell them I was under investigation by the cops. Anything, but he made sure I never slept with another black man. He wanted me to be a slave, Jamie, and he finally broke me, I guess."

I was desperate to compare notes. "What's it like, Rocco?"

"It's hell, just hell. Sometimes he'll bring home that other guy Tom." I nodded to show him I knew who Tom was. "Well, they'll break into the house and they'll start this game thing they do. They'll pick some time in history and make believe that they're living in that period. I have to figure out what it is and who I'm supposed to be. It's always something racial. Like last week they came in and they were making like we were in Africa and that I was a white slaver they had captured. They were supposed to be tribal chiefs. Brendan put on this real heavy, real primitive music. And they were wearing African clothes. They used my body to make up for all the African children that had ever been sold off to America as slaves.

"And another time Brendan brought by these four other cops. They were all black and all had dicks that could kill you. They made believe I was a dope pusher who was selling heroin in the ghetto and ruining the lives of black teenagers. They took their revenge by gang-banging me, one after another, till each one had fucked me at least twice. I was bleeding for days.

"He's always pulling things like that, Jamie. Every night when we listen to the news, if there's anything on the tube that tells about a white person doing something to a black person, I get it—I get fucked, or he ties me up and goes to find people to work me over, or he'll take me to a backroom bar where I have to suck off every single black person there."

83

My eyes were watering as I thought about Rocco's plight. The poor guy, trapped by love, forced to do all these perverted acts. I thought he was going to cry, too. But I had misjudged; those weren't tears. "Oh, Jamie," he said, turning to face me finally, "it's all wonderful." The look on Rocco's face was the glazed expression of a totally satisfied man. One who had found his own private key to happiness.

Rocco's tempo picked up as he catalogued all the things that he and Brendan had been doing. And then I told him about Mr. Benson. We talked about the strange feelings of satisfaction and security I had been experiencing. Rocco understood.

"I know, Jamie, it's the same for me. I still work a couple nights a week—just nights that Brendan has to work himself, because we need more money than he makes. I give him my paycheck and I just use my tips for subways and cigarettes and stuff. But he makes all the decisions, and as hard as it is to keep up with his moods and his wild sex stuff, still I feel better since I finally gave in and said I'd be his boy. I don't know about it as much as you seem to—I mean about being someone's boy—but it's the trip Brendan's on and if that's what he wants, I'll do it. It does make me feel secure though. It feels good to have someone want you so much that you don't have to feel funny about wanting them a lot."

"Then, Rocco, why did you warn me off? Why did you try to keep me from going home with Mr. Benson that first night? Did you really think I couldn't handle it?"

Rocco was quiet for a minute; he was trying to decide whether or not to tell me something. Finally he said, "Jamie, some men who go home with the Topmen...they never come back."

"What do you mean?" I was shocked.

"They never find any bodies, but they never come back. They just disappear."

I couldn't understand that. How did Rocco know this? Could Mr. Benson be involved? What could be happening to the ones who disappeared?

"Brendan doesn't want to admit it. But he knows it's true."

Before I could get out another question, Brendan's voice boomed out. "Boy!" And Rocco jumped up and ran from the kitchen.

FIVE

When Rocco returned to the kitchen, we continued comparing notes about our masters and our new lives. The booming voices from the other room would command the presence of one or the other of us occasionally—getting cups of coffee or refills in their brandy glasses. Rocco and I tried to piece their conversation together.

"Jamie, they're worried about the missing guys. I know it." He had just reported an exchange the two masters had been having about Porytko, the Polish Topman, and about how dumb he was. Rocco said that Mr. Benson had commented: "He's so stupid, he might be the one pulling this off."

Did Rocco agree? "No, Jamie, it can't be Porytko; these guys who disappear, they're all beautiful, really good looking. They wouldn't go home with a slob like that." I pointed out that some men had strange taste. "No, Jamie, Porytko's out. It can't be him."

My mind was reeling from the new idea of real danger being associated with my slavery. "Rocco, why did you think it was Mr. Benson?"

"I didn't, Jamie; it's just that he's so handsome, and he used to pick up so many men. Well, I just never knew. It's hard to figure out just who it would be, since they share so many slaves."

"They do?"

"Hasn't he given you to anyone yet?"

"No, he just talked about my being available."

"Well, they pass us around a lot. I'm afraid you'll have to get used to it. They have these rules, that everyone's slave is available to the others. I guess Mr. Benson's been keeping you at home for training, but if you're in the clubhouse, any one of them can use you."

I shuddered, remembering that one night I had gone there and had been branded.

"Especially if they just trick, they'll pass the man along to whoever wants someone. So you can't tell just by who picks someone up. You have to know who saw him last. And we can't ask them!"

The other conversation was beyond our hearing:

"Brendan, it has to be Hans. There's no one else who would be capable. And that bastard's so mean…"

"I know, Mr. Benson, but how are we ever going to prove it? I'm worried. If the police ever come into this, if they put all the pieces together, they'll find the Topmen and blow the whole thing. We have to take care of it ourselves. And I'm concerned not just because of the club. Look, Mr. Benson, I'm a cop, and I'm proud of it. I'm withholding information from an investigation. Not only am I putting myself in jeopardy, I'm denying my pledges to the force. I've got to find out what's at the bottom of all this."

"Do you think it's murder?"

Brendan thought for a while. "I hope not, but we have to be prepared for it. It could be. If it's not, then what? There've been twenty guys who've disappeared in two months. The investigators are so blinded by prejudice that they haven't seen the obvious pattern. But I have. I know they've all been in leather bars when they were last seen. I know it, and I know that they all were last seen with members of our club. But I can't trace them further unless I come out in the open with my information. I can't convince anybody with the circumstantial evidence I have now. And to accuse a club member without proof is going to be more difficult than to convince a jury. The guys like Hans. They think he's okay. Everyone is so into our concept of brotherhood that they'd defend him unless I had overwhelming proof."

"We could set someone up."

"I've thought of that, Mr. Benson, but we don't know anything about what happens...later. We don't know where he takes them, or what he does with them. I've tailed him many times. I've never seen him with one of the boys, and I've never seen him go anywhere but home to his apartment or over to Jersey City to his office. I can't let anyone take that chance."

"What about one of us?"

Brendan dismissed the idea. "Who's going to take one of us for bottoms?"

Just then, I brought in a new bottle of brandy that Mr. Benson had ordered. The two men watched me so intently that I thought they were going to pounce on me, and didn't know whether to stay or leave. When nothing was said, I went back into the kitchen.

"Rocco, they've gotten real strange now. They just stared at me without saying a word."

"They must have been waiting for you to leave, that's all. I tell you Jamie, they're really worried about this."

"No, Brendan, I won't send Jamie into that without more information. We have to discover what happens.

You say Hans never goes anywhere but home or to the office…" Mr. Benson pondered that for a while.

Mr. Benson closed the door after Rocco and Brendan had left. My mind wasn't allowed to linger on the strange tales of missing men. The look on Mr. Benson's face had something different in mind.

"Go clean yourself out."

Even a couple of hours visiting with an old friend hadn't let me forget who I was to this man, my master. The cold glint in his eye showed me he hadn't forgotten either. "Yes, Sir."

I went off to the bathroom and set up the equipment. In a few minutes I was gushing warm liquid up my bowels, getting ready for Mr. Benson. I was thinking about him. When I was with Mr. Benson and paying attention to him, I had no room in my mind for anyone or anything else.

I was thinking about how much I had changed. I looked down at the nugget-hard nipples on my chest, at the expanded jockstrap covering my shaved crotch, and I felt the brand on my ass. Owned lock, stock and barrel by someone else. Irrevocably marked as chattel, a possession. And it was becoming increasingly clear to me that it had been my choice, that this was a man I had chosen all along the way. From the opening night in the bar to this act of cleaning out my body for his pleasure, I had decided to make myself over for Mr. Benson. To give up the day-to-day freedoms of a meaningless life for the sake of belonging to something, someone, in order to belong to Mr. Benson.

The douching was part of one of our rituals. One of the set of actions that ground in the reality of my subservience, one of the ways Mr. Benson had devised to show both of us that I was ready and willing to do his bidding.

It didn't come as regularly as the polishing of his toilet, or the shaving of my body. But it was more menacing. It was no slight social convention. It took our life deeper into a reality of its own.

When the water came out of me as cleanly as it had gone in, I knew I was ready. I wiped myself off and went into his bedroom where, as I knew he would be, Mr. Benson was waiting.

He was naked. He stood there, the hair over his cock and balls emphasized by my own lack of covering. I was overcome by the sight of him. The chest, the full, muscled stomach, the arms promising such strength. Mr. Benson, my master, my man, the one for whom I would do anything. I went to him that night as I had on other nights and knelt before my living idol. Waiting for him, barely able to restrain myself and my emotions.

"Take it, boy."

I greeted the most welcome of commands with a lunge at the cock that had begun the whole thing. I took its uncut length into my mouth and sucked quietly and lustily at its salty shaft, delighting at the smell of the hair over the crotch. My hands went up and gently lifted the full hanging balls, their silky weight always a pleasure to me. My mind went through somersaults, thinking about Mr. Benson and the manhood of his that was pulsing down my throat. The pleasure was short lived. As soon as he was hard, Mr. Benson pulled back.

"Put on my chaps."

I got off the floor and went over to the bed where the black leather waited for me. I picked up the covering and returned to him. First, I pulled the waistband around him and snapped it in place. Then I struggled with the zipper until it caught, first on one leg, then on the other. Then I slowly pulled each one down the width of his thighs and past his knees and over the bulge of his calves. I leaned back. Mr. Benson was one of those men who wore leather naturally, one of those studs that everyone else tries to be like. There was no façade about Mr. Benson when he had on his chaps. They were as natural a part of his being as the hair on his head.

My cock was standing straight out from my body as I looked up at him. I thought of gladiators in their armor, ready to go into battle. There was Mr. Benson, clothed for the arena where he was about to take me, the slave boy, in front of the crowds.

"Get the grease."

I went to the night table and brought back the can of Crisco. He put out his arm. I opened the container and scooped out a handful of the white lubricant. I started with his wrist, laying on a thick glob, and then spread it up and down the forearm, through the knuckles and over each of the fingers. I left a coating on every part of his arm up to his elbow. I rubbed it in until the warmth of his body melted the whiteness into a shining oil covering his skin. Mr. Benson was ready. It was my turn.

Mr. Benson liked offerings. He, like some ancient god, measured obedience by the size of sacrifice. Whenever something was to be done to me, Mr. Benson let me do as much of the preparation as possible. I knew it was time, as I silently went over to where the cuffs were kept. I came back and knelt once more in front of him. I put on the two wristcuffs, the hooks dangling in front of them. Then I reached down and fastened the ankle bands. Mr. Benson took his ungreased hand and, with my help, snapped each of my wrists to one of my ankles. I was bound and waiting for him. He gently pushed me over onto my back into a position where I was forced to spread my legs, the metal attaching each of my wrists to an ankle making me expose my asshole to him. My cock rubbed painfully against the tight pouch of my jockstrap.

The greased hand came down and warm, oily fingers started to massage the hole. I could almost count them as they spread open the circle of muscle. I quickened my breath as they shoved up against the sphincter. I moaned as the knuckles followed, and bit my tongue in the face of the wave of pain turning to pleasure as the widest part of his hand went into me, and then it was there, his whole hand deep inside me, pulling away at the very being and center of my body, grabbing my soul.

That immeasurable sensation of Mr. Benson holding on to the center of my bowels swept over me. I looked right at him, my mouth gaping open as he talked to me. "My good little ass-boy. My good little slave. Learning to take Mr. Benson every way he wants you."

The strong muscles of his arm pumped away at me, my stomach contracted against the force, my mind pushed back, trying to greet this man of men, trying to please Mr. Benson.

He was stroking away at his cock, the hard pole of manhood covered with the looseness of his foreskin. Mr. Benson, my master, was whacking away at his own sex while he pumped away at me. We never could last long at these scenes we both loved so much, and his white semen soon shot out over my body, my open mouth fighting to take the ooze, trying to eat the man who grabbed at my being with a hot fist shoved deep inside me.

My life with Mr. Benson took on a growing meaning with almost every passing day. I was more and more aware of how much I had given up to him and how much I was vulnerable to him for my existence. I had no job, I had no money of my own, I had no home of my own. I was totally dependent on him, and my mind was totally dependent on my trust of him.

"That's one of the things that makes the disappearance of these other guys so horrible, Jamie. SM, whether it's the real thing that you and Mr. Benson do or the sex play thing that Brendan and I do, it's something that needs trust and demands care. These guys are all into leather. They've trusted someone and they've been taken advantage of at their moment of least defense."

Rocco had become adamant the next Sunday that he came over with Brendan. "We've got to do something."

"What can we do?"

"Jamie, they're our brothers. They're like *us*. They're taking the risk to live out their real selves. If *we* desert them, there's no hope for them."

"But, Rocco, what can we do? I'm kept here without any clothes; I haven't been let out of the apartment in over a month now. I couldn't *do* anything if I *knew* what it should be."

"There's a way, Jamie. Next week there's a Topmen party. Mr. Benson must be ready to take you to one; he's let Brendan come here twice now. That's going to be our first chance. After that, you're going to have to get him to take you more often. Here's what we're going to do..."

"Brendan, I tell you every time I look at Jamie and think about that poor guy in the hands of someone who would mistreat him, it just sends me up the wall. What kind of pervert would play top and then kidnap a little guy like that? It's getting to me, Brendan. We have to do something. There's a party next weekend. That's going to be our chance.

Brendan nodded.
"Here's what we're going to do…"

I wasn't at all sure about Rocco's idea. But there was a possibility. I wasn't convinced I'd be able to go through with it—even after I knew that Mr. Benson would be taking me to the party—until Thursday night. What happened then made me want to do it, but for totally different reasons.

"Boy, we're going to have company at nine o'clock."

I looked up from the book I was reading in the corner and waited for Mr. Benson to explain. Brendan and Rocco had been the only guests up till then. "Come here. I want to talk to you about it."

Puzzled, I went over to Mr. Benson and rested my head against his outstretched hand. "Boy, there are some things that just shouldn't exist in slaves. Things like contentiousness, resistance, you know that, don't you, boy?"

"Yes, Sir." My only acts that approached having fought back to Mr. Benson had been crying for mercy when he had strung me up to "exercise" my tits.

"Boy, another trait that should be wiped out of a slave's mind is jealousy. A slave should never be jealous of his master. Once the two of them have made their contract, they should trust one another to live it out. Do you trust me, boy?"

I didn't like the drift of this conversation at all. I just looked up at him and slowly nodded an agreement I wasn't sure of.

"Boy, another bottom is going to come here tonight. One master can easily take care of two slaves. There's no reason for one of them to feel like he's less than the other. *I will not tolerate*"—those words were heavily emphasized—"*jealousy between*

slaves. I want you to treat the new boy just as tender-
ly as you treat Rocco. Do you understand?"

I knew I didn't like this conversation. My mind
sped as I tried to take in what he was telling me. I
voiced one predominant concern. "Is he going to live
here?"

"No." Mr. Benson smiled as warmly as I ever saw
him smile to me. "You don't have to worry. He's a
trick. Someone I've seen and I'm giving a little training to." His voiced hardened. "If I wanted another
slave to live here, I would have one. But right now
this is just a one-night stand."

I was relieved, a little.

"But I expect you to make it a *very* pleasant night
for me. If you don't, your friend"—he lifted up the
riding crop I thought had been retired—"is going to
have a few words with you later. Now go clean yourself out. I want you ready for whatever happens
tonight."

I wasn't in the best mood as I douched, thinking
about another bottom coming to see Mr. Benson. But
my time with Mr. Benson had already changed my
head so much that my thoughts went rapidly from
concern and worry to intrigue and excitement.
Another slave? What would he be like? What was
the sex going to be like? I started to get hot thinking
of watching Mr. Benson taking care of another man.

By the time I was finished and went into the living
room I was really turned on. I was ready for Mr.
Benson's surprise evening plans. I found him waiting
in the chair by the fireplace. He had put on his full
Topmen uniform—leather pants, khaki shirt, smartly
polished boots, cap. He was gorgeous and I was
horny. I went over to him and knelt before his
beloved figure, hoping that maybe I could entice him
into a quick suck before the new guy arrived.

Mr. Benson had other ideas. He looked at his watch. I had to suppress a sigh of disappointment as he led me to the familiar hooks in the walls. He put on the cuffs and I found myself spread-eagled against the brick surface.

I didn't have to wait long. The doorbell rang and Mr. Benson, *my* master, went to answer it.

The door opened. Silence. The signals had all been prearranged, I guessed.

A man I recognized from pictures plastered all over magazine ads and billboards walked in wearing jeans and a flannel shirt and work boots. This man, blond, muscular, with piercing blue eyes and a mustache that was more famous than the Arrow shirts eye patch fell to his knees and kissed my master's boots, silently waiting for instructions.

Everything became much easier for me to take! My master was training one of New York's foremost models to be a slave. And I was going to watch. My crotch started to give its customary pulsing response.

"Stay on your knees and take off the boots and the shirt." Mr. Benson's voice had that quiet, thorough sound of authority I had become accustomed to but had only heard used on me. The tall blond man struggled with the uncomfortable position and pulled off his boots. His lips—luckily for him—kept moving on the slick surface of my master's leather while he blindly found the buttons of his shirt. He was still there, mouth on Mr. Benson's foot, when the shirt came off and only the tight blue jeans covered his body.

There was a thick covering of blond chest hair. I wondered if he were going to be able to keep it tonight. Or was Mr. Benson going to shave him? There was a growing lump in his jeans. Was Mr. Benson going to let him relieve that horrible pressure? What was Mr. Benson going to do?

I was surprised when he pulled a dog leash out of his pocket. I had worn one only the first night I went to the Topmen Club. Mr. Benson reached down and attached it to the kneeling Adonis' neck. He jerked up with the handle: "Up, but only on all fours." The blond complied. Mr. Benson led him over to where I was silently strung up.

"Look at this, slave. Here's what a well-trained boy does for his master. Are you willing to try to be as good as this boy?"

"Yes, Sir." The blond's voice was low and respectful.

"This is your brother slave. He is a student who has gone the distance you are going to have to go. Does that excite you?"

"Yes, Sir." The model could barely mumble the words. I remembered the terrifying feeling of admitting those desires for the first time. And the wondrous release of having been able to say them.

Mr. Benson's hand came to the strap of my jock and pulled it down to reveal the nude skin underneath it. "This is what happens to someone who becomes a slave. Do you know you're beginning the path that will leave you like this? Wanting this? Needing this?"

The kneeling figure could barely be heard. "Yes, Sir."

"Rub your face in this slave's crotch. You are the junior here. Show him the respect your superior deserves." Mr. Benson's pull on the leash was sharp and the face was suddenly buried in my groin, my now fully hard cock jutting out, desperate for the feel of his mouth, but I was never expecting the next words to come from Mr. Benson. "Suck it."

For the first time since I had met Mr. Benson, someone's mouth closed over my hard prick. I fought to keep my orgasm back. Luckily, Mr. Benson meant this only as a ritual. I was relieved when he dragged that warm, moist opening away from me. I looked down at the nameless man, realizing that I had never dreamt of having my cock sucked by anyone that famous or beautiful.

Mr. Benson undid the hooks and I found myself supporting myself on stiff legs. "Kneel, boy."

I got on my knees and was facing the new man. Looking right into his eyes and recognizing the combination of fear and anticipation that had been mine when I first met this master.

"Kiss him, boy." My lips went out and found the firm mouth of the blond. Our eyes stayed open; the man didn't know how to respond. I acted blindly to Mr. Benson's commands, just as I had been ordered to.

"That's mighty pretty, boys. The good slave boys kissing one another nice and soft. Getting themselves ready for their man."

Mr. Benson's talking during sex always gave me clues about the direction he was heading. and I could sense this one. My jockstrap was stuck down around my knees. I reveled in the strange feeling of the freedom of my prick as it pushed against the denim fabric of the pants in front of me.

"Stand up." Abruptly we both rose. "Jamie, take off your jockstrap and then remove his pants." There was that tone in Mr. Benson's voice that let me know that he was getting turned on. My jock fell off easily. I reached over and took the unbelted jeans and undid the zipper. I pushed them over his round hips and nearly jumped back with surprise as an enormous and perfectly shaped circumcised cock leapt out at me. I nearly forgot myself and went down on it, but I got hold and slid the jeans off his calves, marveling at the softness of the down covering his legs from crotch to ankle. It was a golden coating, never thick enough to be described as "hairy," more like a fuzz that mellowed the sharp definition of his legs.

I was swept into the smell of his crotch. Mr. Benson hardly ever wore underpants, and this was another renewed delight—the odor of sweaty balls caught in the cotton briefs. I had to bite back my tongue again before it acted on its own.

The model stepped out of the pile of clothing I left at his feet. Once again we were staring at one another; if anything, the intensity of his concern had increased.

"You are both my slaves. I expect you to respect that and me. You"—he suddenly turned to the blond—"are the apprentice. This is an advanced student, I expect you to have respect for his learning. And you"—he turned to me—"I expect you to help this initiate. I expect you both to work only for my satisfaction. Do you both understand?"

"Yes, Sir." Our answers came in unison.

"Feel his shaved crotch. Take a good feel at the body of a slave." My skin tingled as the warm and unaccustomed hand came up and spread itself over my neglected balls, lifting them up as his palm spread over the smooth skin. I was going through new highs. A new depth of pride overtook me. I was feeling the emotions of a soldier in an army as a new recruit looks on and sees the completeness of his training, knowing that, if he can last it out, he too can qualify to wear the uniform.

The blond's eyes were wide with amazement at the strange feeling of a hairless body against his hands. "His ass too." The hand went under my crotch and felt my naked asshole; a finger pressed against the opening. The blond's cock, bigger even than Mr. Benson's, waved in the air before me, the feel of my body and sight of my surrender as I spread open my legs to allow his entry obviously affecting him.

"I want to see my boys get along well. On the floor!" The last sentence was a sudden command. We dropped down and automatically lay on our backs. "Your heads on each other's cocks!" We scurried again and suddenly I was faced with the reality of that enormous prick with big hanging balls covered with that yellow fuzz. "Suck." I gobbled the thick piece down, almost immediately gagging on its girth, and on my greed. Again, the shocking sensation of someone else's throat taking my cock swept through my system.

I was so taken by the smells of the sweaty crotch that I forgot what Mr. Benson might be doing until I felt his hands roughly joining mine behind the guy's waist with a pair of cuffs and a snap. I could hear him repeat the movement with the other man's hands and felt his arms tighten around me. The leash from his collar was brought down and fastened to my cuffs; something else came around my wrists and pulled up against my skin.

We were tied in that position! In no more than a minute I was trapped with that man's prick in my throat. I had enough experience with Mr. Benson to know that more was coming, and the quick fiery pain across my ass let me know I was right. A belt? A paddle? A strap? He had them all. His legs straddled our joined bodies and from the sounds I knew he was going from my ass to the other slave's, forcing each of us to shove his cock down the back of the other's throat with each blow. The red warmth of my ass spread as the number of whacks mounted up. There were no words, just the muffled groans from each of us as the leather returned time and again to visit our quickly burning flesh.

Tears had formed in my eyes when Mr. Benson finally stopped. The gulps of the blond's throat pressing against my hard cock let me know his own were flowing too.

The rough hands of Mr. Benson untied us as quickly as they had bound us to one another. "Don't move." The order kept my mouth on the model's prick and my own shaft down his neck. Mr. Benson walked away from us. The sounds told me he was sitting in his favorite chair.

"Jamie, up on your knees." I gently pulled out of the man's mouth, leaving behind plenty of pre-come. I lifted myself into a sitting position.

"You, on your hands and knees, back to Jamie." The other man was gently trying to get air into his lungs, fighting back the tears. He moved onto all fours and left me with a clear view of the mounds of his ass streaked with red welts and of the hole, sharply pink in contrast to the light yellow of his body and its covering.

"Jamie, your master is going to fuck that slave's asshole. He wants it nice and clean and wet. Get in there, boy, and clean that ass for your master."

I looked at the brilliant red stripes across the pale complexion, and at the puckered skin in the middle of the crevice between his cheeks. My hand went up and pulled apart the mounds, lifting the opening up to meet my mouth.

The taste of the sweat was clean. The hints of the asshole's own sweet flavor led me to push my tongue up and into him, licking the surfaces of the suddenly hairless membrane inside, slurping up spit to lubricate the circle of muscular flesh. *My man's going to shove his prick up here!* My cock went hard as steel thinking about the meaty shaft poking into this warm, moist hole. Spit flowed out of my mouth, down the crack around the ass, dripping off his tight balls now lifting themselves up into his body.

Mr. Benson came around behind me and slapped an encouragement on my backside. "Get it good and wet, Jamie; get him good and ready." I felt Mr. Benson pulling on his dick, the foreskin moving up and down the length.

Another slap on my ass! "Move out, Jamie, I'm going to fuck this asshole."

I jumped out of the way as Mr. Benson stepped in closer and put the wide head up to the blond's pink muscle. The model tried to pull away. A sharp whack of Mr. Benson's hand on his ass brought him back to reality. "Stay on your knees or I'll tie you up."

The thickly muscled legs moved back to meet Mr. Benson. I watched the beautiful tension on the arms as they pressed against the floor, holding up not only his own weight but my master's as well. I could see sweat collecting on his biceps as they bulged out from the strain; I watched the stomach muscles contract as they attempted to keep from faltering.

Unthinkingly, I moved over and ran my tongue to slop up the sweat on his body, the salt taste making me want more. I kept at it with long, slow strokes. The model moaned in appreciation as I lapped up his fluid. I kept celebrating as the ridge of developed muscles hardened. "That's a good boy, Jamie. Make him feel good. Make him glad he's got my prick inside him." Mr. Benson was gasping from the savage fucking he was giving the man. His whole body was slamming into the open, exposed figure before him, making him use every one of the strained muscles to defend himself against the onslaught.

"Get his dick!"

I went down on the floor on my back and slid beneath the grunting bodies as the walloping continued above me. The blond's cock was hard! The enormous stick swung in the air over me; I strained to lift my neck up to greet it. I drew it in, timing myself to meet one of Mr. Benson's thrusts.

"Jesus Christ!" the model exclaimed as the wide prickhead disappeared into my throat, shoving itself with a desperate need for release. The moans started to increase; the thrusts came more quickly. I could see the blond pushing harder back to meet Mr. Benson's pelvis as it slammed forward into him.

"Jesus Christ! Christ Jesus!" The man was screaming. Mr. Benson started to give the signaling shouts of impending joy, and there it was! A thick, gooey spurt of come flowing down my throat. And another! Too much! It came out the side of my mouth and down my chin. No matter how quickly I tried to swallow, it flowed over my lips and onto my chest.

They stayed arched over me for minutes. The huge dick in my mouth barely had begun to deflate when Mr. Benson pulled out, his own wonderful cock suddenly popping into my view, coming down to press against the blond-fuzzed balls in front of me, almost able to join the tool in my mouth.

Mr. Benson stood. "Get up."

The remark was meant for me. I came out from under the body of the model and stood beside him facing Mr. Benson. "Jamie, how'd you like a piece of this nice ripe ass?" I couldn't understand the question. "Do you want to fuck him?"

I looked down at the body straddling the floor. This man was one of the most desired males in New York City. He had the kind of body that existed only in ads for designer underwear. He stayed on his hands and knees with his head dangling submissively.

"Yes, Sir." My answer was almost a whisper.

"It's all nice and greased with my come, boy, go

ahead in." Mr. Benson sat on the couch on the other side of the blond's waiting body. My prick strained with its own weight as I went behind him and once again studied the beautiful ass. It was standing right up in the air; his legs had been spread apart by Mr. Benson's hammering. The balls, now relaxed after orgasm, swung low away from his body with that fine blond-hair covering. The red marks on his mounds still stood out in stark contrast to the pale skin.

I took my hard shaft and poked at his hole. He moaned slightly; was it from pain or anticipation? I hadn't fucked anyone for months. It's hardly my forte. But here it was, the chance to stick it into one of America's most beautiful men. The opening was wet, and I slid past the barely resisting ring of muscle. A loud gasp of air came from both of us. And I started pumping at the incredible warmth of his body, grabbing hold of the firm waist, watching the sharp triangles of muscle on his sides.

"That's right, boy, fuck that slave's ass." Mr. Benson's hand came out and whacked encouragement on my cheeks. "Slam it in."

My pumping became harder, my thrusts came more quickly, the thought of the man's come dripping out of my mouth while I watched Mr. Benson's prick grinding into him burst out into my own orgasm quickly and violently. I shot my load deep inside his gorgeous ass, growling in victory, and receiving another hard whack from Mr. Benson.

I stayed inside him quietly. Amazed at myself for getting so hot over fucking someone and waiting for Mr. Benson to give a new order, I looked over at him. He was clothed in his uniform; the strong arms were crossed over his chest. Mr. Benson looked very pleased.

"Okay, Jamie, pull out of him and go shower. I

want to talk to this slavemeat alone." My cock popped out of him. I jumped up and went to the shower room and quickly got under the warm and full flow of water. I felt foolish for my misgivings, however brief, of having a second slave in the house. Now it all seemed hot and wonderful and I wondered when it could happen again. I liked the idea of someone else listening to Mr. Benson talk about me: his number-one slave. It was an affirmation I appreciated feeling.

I remember that, under that shower, I was as happy to be Mr. Benson's slave as I ever would be.

When I returned to the living room, the blond was on his hands and knees—fully dressed this time—kissing Mr. Benson's feet. I must have missed the final command, because he got up and left without a word.

Mr. Benson and I stood at opposite ends of the room as the man put on a sheepskin jacket over his flannel shirt—it was a quick vision of a cigarette ad when the whole outfit was on—and then he left.

I looked over to Mr. Benson. "Come here, boy."

I went over to him and followed the order in his eye to drop to my knees. He reached over and took the back of my neck, pulling my face into his crotch, rubbing it against the leather-covered bulge.

"You're a good boy, Jamie. You're learning very quickly. I like that. We'll have to find a way to reward you soon."

I put my arms around my master's legs and embraced him, thinking then that I needed no greater reward than that—to be with him.

I had no way of knowing what Mr. Benson had planned for me.

SIX

Mr. Benson had never mentioned the party. I knew about it only from Rocco. We had assumed that I would be taken along. On Saturday, I kept waiting for Mr. Benson to say something. The later it got, the more excited I became—I thought Mr. Benson must be planning to spring it on me as part of a sex trip—and Mr. Benson's sex trips were always a joy.

Finally at about nine o'clock that night, he called me over. "You know by now that trust is the cornerstone to a good SM relationship, don't you? And you've learned to trust me, haven't you?" I nodded to both statements. "Go over to the coat closet and bring out the packages."

Puzzled, but still convinced this was all part of a scene, I went to the storage area and pulled out three bulky store packages. I took them over to where Mr. Benson stayed sitting. "Open them."

I took off the three covers in rapid succession; my head swam in a wondrous wave of leather scent. The boxes were full of black skins. What was this?

"Put them on, Jamie."

Leather! Mr. Benson had brought me leather. I ripped the clothes out of their containers and pulled on a pair of wonderfully tight pants that lifted my jockstrapped crotch up into an enticing lump. I fell on the floor and struggled to pull the heavy engineer boots over my feet, and then back up again to slip on the black jacket, my chest skin contrasting with the ebony of the leather.

"There's more." I went through the paper packing material and my hand found a leather motorcycle cap.

Mr. Benson was enjoying my enthusiasm. "Go look at yourself in the mirror." I bolted over to the full-length glass Mr. Benson keeps in his room. The image was striking. I thought again about how much I had changed in the past few months. There I was, a black knight, just like the ones I used to chase. With one difference—from the right side of the leather pants and from the right shoulder of the jacket came short but heavy loops of chain. The symbols of my clothing were to be as permanent as the life I was leading.

Mr. Benson had followed me in and circled me, pulling at a band here, feeling the fit of the jacket there. "It's much better than I would have thought—it was a risk to have it made without a fitting—but you look fine, just fine.

"Come back into the other room. I want to talk to you about something."

When we were back, I stood in front of him and listened to his orders. My excitement quickly paled.

"You know what I just said about trust? Well, Jamie, I'm going to ask you to do something this weekend that involves a great deal of trust. Jamie, I'm going to give you some money. I want you to go away until Tuesday morning. Think of it as a vacation. Take a room in a nice hotel. Live off room service if you want. But I don't want you here."

Who ever heard of a slave using room service? I didn't like the sound of this one bit. Suddenly I was being given clothes—so what if they were leather—and a ticket to leave. But what could I say? No? What would happen if I rebelled and wouldn't leave? The answer flashed through my mind as quickly as the question had: I would be thrown out.

I was in a jam. Trust, he said. He was the master. Why wasn't I trusting him? Was I deep down inside just another jealous fairy? I knew that's what he'd think if I gave in to the feelings inside me that wanted to resist.

"You want me to leave right now?"

"Yes." Mr. Benson almost looked concerned. "Jamie, you just have to trust what I'm doing. I know best. Go on a holiday, have a good time, and come back on Tuesday."

I couldn't keep the tear from coming out the corner of one eye. I was jealous. I knew, I just knew...this had to do with that model. But I had little choice. I tried to conjure up as much as I could of the emotions that had led me to this place—a slave standing in front of his master.

He gave me an absurdly large amount of money and rang for the elevator. "You'll understand when it's all done, Jamie," he said as the door opened on our floor.

"Yes, Sir," I mumbled to him, and nodded a slight greeting to Tom.

As the cage went down in the building, I turned to Tom and asked, "Do Mr. Benson's slaves ever get holidays, Tom?"

The big black man smiled and said, "Boy, no slave of Mr. Benson ever had time off I know of. You must be doing something right!" Or something *very wrong*, I thought to myself.

It had been weeks since I had been let out of the apartment. I hit Fifth Avenue and suddenly realized that I was free, free to do anything I wanted. There had been no restrictions imposed, no taboos. I could go anywhere, say anything, see anything. I panicked. I hadn't made those decisions for weeks. What was I going to do? Where was I going to go?

I needed a place to spend the night. My new life had taken over so completely that I almost didn't notice people's stares at me as I walked down the Avenue. I had to stop for a minute to remember that a man in full black leather wasn't always an everyday occurrence. Where would I stay the night in this outfit? Shit, if I was going to be put out of my own home with a wad of money, I might as well enjoy it. I'd go to a hotel, a good hotel. But not in these clothes.

I thought for a minute and then hurried over to Seventh Avenue, hoping the leather stores would still be open. I was lucky and found one.

The store had what I wanted—a tan uniform shirt and a black leather tie. I took them off the rack of the store and put them on as I paid for them, using a small mirror on the counter to do the tie. It was still heavy leather, the clerk's interested glances kept me aware of that; but it would also probably get me past a few doormen. I was hoping that jaded New York would see the leather pants as chic, and be willing to acknowledge the tie as the necessary part of a passable dress.

I had been so anxious to get to the store before it closed and to find the right things there that I hadn't paid any attention to the other people in the shop. And I had only paid the least possible attention to the clerk.

"That's a good look, kid." His voice was deep and laced with a slight accent. Italian? I took my gaze away from the mirror and turned to him. What a hunk. Deep black eyes, thick black hair, a rough shaved beard and a heavy moustache flowing down over his upper lip. The sleeves of his red flannel shirt were rolled up over hair-covered forearms, heavy with muscle. I looked down and saw an impressive lump in his tight faded jeans, its size accentuated by clinging chaps, and his character hinted at by a big link of metal holding keys on the left side of his waist.

It was a sharp jolt. I had been so concerned with Mr. Benson's strange behavior and then so worried about time that I hadn't really prepared myself for the possibility of sex with another man. Did I want it? Was I going to avoid it? What should I do? I blurted out a quick thanks to buy time; it only got me a long stare as his eyes went up and down my body, slowly sizing it up. "The store closes in about half an hour. Want to meet me for a drink?"

I stuttered and stammered and finally answered with a shrug. "Sure." This was supposed to be a holiday.

I left quietly after he gave me the name of the nearest leather bar. I only hoped that this guy was going to be a more successful adventure than Larry and his gleaming white jockstrap and his fantasies of buddy fucking.

In the familiar bar, I got a drink and stood against the wall. I thought of how relieved I was not to have to go to places like this anymore. It was just another way that living with Mr. Benson had proven to be important to me. Going out and looking for sex was something I no longer had to do. Well, tonight, anyway, sex had come looking for me.

After nearly two months' absence, the bar looked good to me, even this early at night. The flannel and leather costumes were familiar. It was actually fun to watch them all and to think of each of them as they went through their moves to circle and hunt one another.

I had been cocky before I met Mr. Benson, but I also know that my cockiness was a cover for a deeper sense of inadequacy. I hadn't really felt that I was attractive enough for all these men. But now, with the assurances of Mr. Benson and the tight grasp of the leather pants on my shaven crotch and the prospect of a stud coming to meet me soon, now I had more assurance. I didn't have to wonder if these men were looking at me. If Mr. Benson would look at me and keep me, then I was worth it. And the nude skin of my body moving against the cool surface of the leather made me more aware of my sex than I had ever been before.

Something else familiar started to go through my mind: I was starting to anticipate the man who had told me to meet him here. Just as I had spent so much time waiting for Mr. Benson that night in the Mineshaft, now I played out all my hopes and fears for the new man. What would his crotch be like? What would his prick be like? Cut? Long, loose fore-skin? Would his body hair cover his ass as thickly as it obviously did his chest? What would he want from me? What did he think when he saw someone like me covered in leather with a link of chain hanging down the right side?

I started to think more and more about the man and less and less about Mr. Benson. That realization startled me. I felt that I was failing somehow. How could I forget Mr. Benson so easily? Did it mean I didn't care for him as much as I had thought?

The sudden appearance of the clerk swept aside my idle thoughts. There he was, a heavy motorcycle jacket over his large body, the black of his jacket and the chaps highlighting even more the triangle of bulge in the denim-clad crotch.

He waved a greeting and went straight over to the bar. Familiar tension shot through my body and I stood up, waiting for him to come over to me. I was surprised when he walked into the back after he had gotten the beer can from the bartender. Was I supposed to follow? Or was he just making a fast trip to the john? I decided to wait. The tension started to produce a flow of sweat from my pits; the moisture heightened the odor of the leather.

Only a few months ago I wouldn't have known what this was about. I would have been insulted by a trick who so casually took me for granted. But now I understood. The probability was that this guy was leaving me standing there on purpose. He was putting me in my place.

When he returned I flashed a smile at him and started to exchange greetings. There wasn't going to be a pleasant social exchange, though. He held out a second can of beer. I hadn't seen him buy two. I was thrown off by his cold stare, and by the beer. I took hold of the can and was shocked by an unexpected warmth coming from the metal. I looked up at him. "I like to get things settled as soon as possible," he said. "No reason to play games."

He leaned back against the wall and looked over the room, leaving me with the silent and secret humiliation of his piss in the can. I stood there, my head hanging down, letting the feelings sink in. Slavemeat. I drank from the new can; the fluid stung as it went down my throat. The acid flow burned its way into my stomach. Slavemeat, drinking piss.

His hand came over and groped at my ass, pulling me to him. My crotch was pressed against his leg. He was still looking out at the crowd, not even glancing at me. The hand went down inside the leather pants and grasped the shaven ass. The sudden contact with the nude skin finally got me a look from him.

"No novice, are you?"

"No, Sir."

"Kneel."

I went down on my knees. I didn't look up to see if any eyes followed my descent. My head had gone into the space created for it by Mr. Benson. I sipped more from the hot can.

A collar came around my neck. From where? How had he known to bring it? Or was he one of those men who always have one—just in case? The leather tightened around my throat; a leash at its end gave slight pressure to its grip.

It had all become so natural. To be there, displayed to the rest of the world. It had become part of me. I was once again waiting for a man to decide what he was going to do with me.

The bar scene was only a prelude. If this guy was putting that much work into setting a mood, there was no hope that the mood was all I was going to get. My crotch rose higher against the leather, filling with its own hopes and dreads about what was to follow.

When he had finished with his beer, the man was obviously ready to move on. He tugged at the leash and led me out of the bar. Even the Village, the most gay part of New York, isn't ready for two leather studs walking the street with a leash joining them. At least not that early in the evening. But this man didn't care about the stares at him, and I knew that he liked the stares at me. They were building with the lingering taste of piss in my mouth to put me where he wanted me.

I was half hard as we went through the streets, the

silent man walking ahead of me holding the promise of a new experience. I studied his body as it moved through the streets with a purposeful, masculine stride. He was taller than Mr. Benson, at least six two. He towered over me. His shoulders were broad, and his legs thick; their curved calves and thighs pressing against the chaps held a promise of firm muscles. His boots were rough with long wear; his leather wasn't new, it had been around awhile.

He suddenly stopped and I waited while he took the ring of keys off his belt and opened the door of a brick building that looked like it must have been converted to housing from industrial space. There were still no words. What would we do when we entered his apartment? Should I complete the role I had accepted and kiss his boots like Mr. Benson would expect me to do? Or should I wait for him to command? Would I be asking for maybe more than I could handle if I gave him that kind of indication?

We went up two flights of narrow stairs and I waited again while he opened locks. My sweat was flowing freely by now. The size of the man, the way he towered over me, the lack of any agreement before I followed him here, they all combined to make me wonder if I was doing something very, very wrong. I felt like a fool. No bottom should just silently follow a man who gives him a can of hot piss and who makes him kneel at the touch of nude flesh.

The door closed behind me with a loud slam. My choices were over. I may have been worried, but I wasn't worried enough to leave. The engorged cock in leather coating was ruling when my head should have been operating.

Whack! A sharp slap hit me full in the face. "Just to keep you going." The smile he gave me was puzzling; the heat on my cheek burned. My cock filled to the breaking point. I was worried, and it loved being worried like this.

He left me standing in the doorway and went over to the other side of the loft space. It was large, almost as large as Mr. Benson's whole apartment. Even if it had been filled with furniture, the pieces would have been lost in the enormity of the room, but it wasn't. There were only a few sparse items: a chair, a desk and a large platform bed sitting in the middle of the area. He pulled out a drawer in the bed's base and took out a piece of leather. He came back over to me. Without warning there was a pair of handcuffs joining my wrists together behind me. And then the leather he carried came up and enveloped my face. There was suddenly no light; I was captured in a sea of darkness. I struggled for air, and finally a small slit opened in front of my nose for me to drag in enough oxygen to keep my consciousness.

The rest of that night was blindness. The whole scene was experienced physically. There were no clear sounds I could hear; there were never any words from the man whose name I didn't even know.

The leather hood was tightened after it had gone on. It must have had straps in the back. My prick grew rock hard with the excitement and danger. I still don't know all of what he did to me that night. I can only reconstruct parts of it.

I was taken away from the doorway into the middle of the space. I think it was the middle. The handcuffs and my clothes were removed. The sudden feeling of air flowing over my body while my head was encased with the blinding material accentuated the sense of nakedness. His hands ran quietly over my skin's surface; they traveled up and down my sides and around my legs. They paused to enjoy the slickness of my hairless ass and to pinch lightly and sharply at my tits, the knobs Mr. Benson had trained to respond to the lightest command. I moaned as his fingers kept turning the nipples, back and forth, both at the same time.

The metal handcuffs were replaced with leather cuffs on my wrists. I thought they must be like Mr. Benson's, but they were softer; there must have been some kind of lining. Then cuffs, again lined, went on my ankles. I was prepared for the handcuffs on my wrists and those on my legs to be joined the way that Mr. Benson used them to bind me. But the man left me standing there for a considerable time and the still-present collar outlined my vulnerability. The mask on my face and the denial of the sense of sight heightened my body awareness. My cock was so hard it touched no part of the rest of me and enjoyed its own flow of cooling air around its protrusion.

When he came back, he started to manipulate my body, positioning it in a way that I couldn't understand. I was desperate to hear his words, but I couldn't have, even if he had spoken to me. The hood was as efficient a silencer as a blinder.

Then there was a shocking tug. Vague mechanical noises came through the hood. And I felt a surge of panic as my legs were pulled out from under me and my arms lifted higher above me. A machine jerked me off the floor; I thought I would have to fall flat on my face, but found the restraints supporting me. When the mechanics stopped I felt like I must have been at a 45-degree angle from the floor, my cock and balls hanging down away from my body, my eyes still unable to tell me what the man was doing.

His hands had taken on a warm feeling as the cool air lowered my own temperature. They returned to me now, starting the soft investigation of theirs. They lingered again at my tits and worked at both of them.

I relaxed a little with the knowledge that he must know what he was doing, and the lining of the leather bands holding me in midair was soft enough to lessen the pain that the job of holding my body could produce. I went into the sensation of his warmth against my nipples; his hands playing with them in an almost gentle way. The turn-on increased as I let my mind stop worrying, and I experienced his quick command of my body.

He left my tits enraged with feeling. The hands traveled down to my crotch. He cupped my balls in one of his palms, and with the other started to play with my cock. He applied an increasing amount of pressure to the vulnerable eggs in their sac, slowly building up to produce a crushing sensation. The balls came together and rolled against one another in his grip. Waves of pain flowed out from them, punctuated by delightful feelings of warmth. My cock was building up to an early orgasm, and just then he stopped, leaving it to wave in the air, leaving it desperate for release.

He walked away again, I think he must have; I couldn't sense his body being nearby. I could only feel the cool air blowing between my stretched legs.

Then he came back. He had grabbed my balls once more and tied something around the base. It felt like leather. I thought at first it was only a cock-ring, but there must have been a great length of it, he kept winding it around and around my scrotum. Every loop I thought he was finished, that he had to be finished, that the sac couldn't stretch any further. When he finally was done, my balls were forced far away from my body by a thick swatch of leather. The pressure was immense—and wonderful.

Another strand started to work its way up my cock. The line of leather wound around the shaft, from the base to just below the head; the tight strands pinched wherever there was a break for the skin to work its way out. I wanted to see! I knew that my cockhead would be full of trapped blood. I wanted to see the redness of the skin as it held back the built-up fluid.

Before I could think more about it, he was back. He started with my nipples once more. Turning them, softly twisting them back and forth. I moaned more and more loudly. Mr. Benson had trained them so well that they responded instantly to his touch, especially with the firm pressure pulling my balls down and keeping my prick so hard.

But again the warm hands were replaced. Cold metal pushed against the oversensitive nipples; gentle pressure built up as they were each attached to clamps that were adjusted to a place just short of intense pain.

Now I was burning with my sex. My cock, my balls, my tits were all bound. I could sense him moving silently behind me. I thought he must be going to fuck me. I could feel him rub his leather against my naked legs. I tried to relax my anus to receive him.

Instead, there came a soft, almost kissing, touch of a belt or strap against my ass. A slow litany of blows started to run up and down each of my legs. The intensity built. He would go all the way down to the bound ankles and climb up one leg, giving even, excruciating taps to the tight ballsac, and linger over my ass, then travel down the other leg only to begin the journey again. Each time the leather traveled over my body, it picked up intensity with its touch.

My moans of pleasure greeted the first journey. They disappeared with the second; by the time he was finished with the third I was shrieking with pain. The whole of my backside below my waist burned

119

with angry welts. Not one inch had been spared. The whole of me pulled against the restraints, fought to release my body from this agony.

I could hardly hear my own screams through the hood. The traveling belt brought out a new one every time it touched me. I had thought I had gone beyond pain with the sessions with Mr. Benson, but I had never experienced anything like this. He must have beaten me with the belt for an hour. When that stopped, I pleaded with him to release me. I couldn't have heard his answer if he spoke one, but I felt his response.

He had moved. Now he began again with the soft strokes of the belt, this time moving over my back. Those first light touches weren't painful at all, but I knew that this meant he was going to repeat the whole performance. I knew that that strip of leather was going to work over my back and my arms just as it had my legs and ass.

By the time another hour had passed, I was reduced to sobbing uncontrollably. He had left my skin so hot and had worked it so much that now even the touch of his soft hand produced floods of horrendous pain.

This must have been what he had wanted. A body racked with pain and deep sobs, one totally at his mercy. I was hardly conscious of feeling him as his cock invaded my ass. My concern was the touch of his hairy and prickled body against the red skin he had left on my backside.

He shoved into me. His body worked back and forth into my ass. The feeling of being fucked was hardly noticed in the whole of the agony of the beating I had received. Vaguely, I was aware when he shot. I could feel the pulsing of his cock as it hardened to pour his come inside me. Again, I hoped it would be over.

I wanted Mr. Benson! I wanted to be freed from this violence and savagery. This wasn't what I wanted! The darkness enveloped me and kept me from seeing him move around after he pulled roughly out of my hole. The fingers went back to my cock and balls. The warm palm again cupped the shaved skin. I stretched my body from the restraints, hopelessly trying to move it away from his cruel grasp. The pressure began to mount on my sac. The balls came together again and rolled against one another. The inside of the hood was wet with my tears as he kept squeezing and manipulating my testicles. Deep growls came up from inside me; the intense pain shifted from my backside to my crotch. The power of the pain in my sac, the small orbs of sex trapped between leather and this man, consumed me.

And then blackness did come.

I had finally given in to the pain. I passed out. I don't know if he even noticed the slackening of my body, or if he cared. When I woke up, I was fully dressed. He had left me against the doorway to his apartment. The roughness of the new fabric of my shirt and the leather on my slacks rasped against the angry skin he had marked so savagely. My body was stiff as I tried to stand. I could barely make it upright. I leaned against the brick wall and looked up at the lit window of the apartment where I had been.

I had met a new kind of top—one who showed his concern and caring by leaving me unconscious in the street, covered with bruises. It wasn't an image I liked. A surge of anger went through me. The asshole hadn't even taken me away from his own building. He didn't care if I complained—to whom? What recourse did a slave have when he had been stupid enough to go home with any leather figure who ordered him to? The police? If I told the people at the store, they'd just laugh. It would probably only enhance his reputation.

Wearily I checked and found the lump of money Mr. Benson had given me. It was still in my pocket.

I wanted to go to bed. My muscles were sore from the exertion they had gone through. They screamed in pain every time I tried to move them. I stumbled somehow to an avenue and hailed a taxi.

The driver looked strangely at me when I slowly put my pained body into the hack. "Where to, bub?"

Where to? A hotel. But which one? I felt the roll of cash in my pocket. Well, he had told me to have a good time. I certainly hadn't started off too well, but maybe I could make up for that. "Take me to the Plaza."

I comforted myself somewhat as the cab sped uptown. The look of the driver's face when I gave him the name of New York's most lavish hotel had been worth the ride itself. I adjusted the tie the sadistic asshole had put on my neck, and smoothed my short hair down as the sights of midtown New York passed by me. We went through the theater district and into the exalted enclaves of the East Side. And there, rising above Central Park on its own block, was the Plaza.

The reservation clerk tried to be suave. I'm sure that two things were on his mind—how did I get in there and how could he get me out—fast. The looks of everyone in the lobby were aimed at my leather. The cap on my head was pushed back, I was holding the heavy jacket over one arm, but the bulging of the leather pants and the press of the uniform shirt were making their own statement. The pain of my skin, the mass of red welts I knew I was going to find there, didn't keep me from putting on a good show. I was going to keep my dignity in front of the pompous clerk and in my own mind.

Besides, however anxious he might have been to get rid of me, the appreciative glances from a couple of the bellboys were more than sufficient compensation.

I had been smart enough to call from a pay booth at the corner—I wasn't going to be told there was no room. He claimed he was having trouble finding the reservation, but hopped to when I suggested I wait on one of the couches across the lobby.

A room was found and two of the bellboys nearly fought with one another to take me up to the floor. I smirked at their enthusiasm and almost forgot the ordeal I had been through until I let my backside brush against the elevator wall.

The room was delightfully large and smelled of a fresh cleaning. I tipped the boy too much and went to the bathroom. It was huge. I turned on the bath water and slowly stripped. When the tub was full, I lowered myself into the water, as hot as I dared. The terrible stripes of red showed against my skin. I sighed deeply as the warmth began to relax the abused muscles. And I thought about the man I had just left and the man I wanted to go back to.

I thought a lot about the relationship I had with Mr. Benson. I had gone through a lot with him and for him. I had done things I had never dreamt I would do. I had been a willing and happy slave to that man. I had been strung up against a wall for his visual pleasure. I had endured his fist in my bowels and his cock in my face for countless hours. I gave all of it to him as a gift and as a sign of my humility and devotion.

This other man—the one without a name—had taken from me savagely. He had beaten me without purpose and had used my body only as he chose. I knew now that what little he had done that I had

123

thought was pleasurable had been done only to make me tolerate more abuse from him. I thought about SM that night. The very idea that there could be rape in an SM context was shocking somehow. But it was obvious that there could be. I thought about that bastard leaving me on a street—for how long? I didn't even really know.

Mr. Benson wouldn't have done that to me.

What was important about Mr. Benson was becoming more and more apparent.

When I finished the bath and stood in the heated, tiled room, drying myself, I had a sudden need to do something for myself. I went, naked, into the bedroom and called room service. They weren't prepared for my order at that time of night, but they'd try.

A half-hour later, a middle-aged waiter got a thrill when I opened the door and let him in with the delivery. I was still naked, with only a towel around my waist. I took the razor I had ordered and tipped him.

Then I went into the bathroom and took off the towel. That night, my first night alone in years, I took the razor and shaved my body. Performing the dedication to Mr. Benson he had requested, but not stopping with my crotch and ass this time, I took off my chest hair and the hair under my arms. I was alone and there was no one there to know what I was doing and what it meant to me, but I knew that Mr. Benson would know when I saw him on Tuesday. I was making love to Mr. Benson, there in that bathroom by myself. My cock jumped at the sight of myself lifting my arms to remove the hair there, the humiliating stance only intensifying the thrill of the action. When it was gone, when my red tits stood out against a hairless background, I dried myself and went to bed. I got into the cool sheets and put a hand up to a sore nipple and with the other hand, I started caressing my hard prick.

I thought about Mr. Benson and the devotion I felt to him. I thought about my love for him and his care for me. I thought about the life I was leading as his slave, and a quick, not-to-be-denied spurt of come came shooting up, stinging the newly shaved skin on my stomach, wetting the sheets so I could sleep, thinking all the time about the presence of Mr. Benson.

SEVEN

I woke the next morning in the splendor of the Plaza. The bright spring sun came through the large windows overlooking Central Park. I was in a surprisingly good mood. I rubbed my hand over the shaven chest and under my arms, my hands gliding over the soft skin, whose surface felt more like silk than human covering.

Mr. Benson! As always nowadays, he was the first thought in my mind. It suddenly dawned on me that I had just slept in a bed for the first time since I had met him. I spread my legs far apart, sliding them over the fresh washed sheets, touching my backside and my balls to the starched fabric. A long, lingering, muscle-stretching yawn came over me as I enjoyed the luxury and tried to ignore my bruises.

If I had been at home, I would have woken to his nudging feet. I would have been sleeping on the floor in my worn bag. But I was alone. The compensation of the luxury accommodations didn't seem to be nearly enough to make up for his absence.

The thought of my man brought on an erection. My shaft stood straight up under the sheets and away from my nude skin. I started to reach down to my cock, but stopped. Mr. Benson didn't like me to beat off in the morning. He liked me to be in need of him. Even if he wasn't here, I decided to stick by the rules. I let the built-up muscle scrape against the cotton and enjoyed my thoughts about Mr. Benson.

That wasn't going to be enough. It was Sunday. I still had two days before I could return to him. I called room service and ordered an outrageous breakfast and the Sunday *Times*. I jumped into the shower and was dry with my leather pants on when the door knock came. I answered quickly.

I had thought the pants and socks I had on were a more modest outfit than the towel around my waist that I had worn when I had called for the razor last night. But there was nothing modest in the stare that greeted me now. Obviously, the leather meant more to this man than the towel would have. And obviously, he wasn't room service.

"I...I was expecting my breakfast," I stammered.

"Maybe you found it," the guttural voice answered. I blushed red at the implications. The man in front of me was about forty. He was handsome in a very rough Italian way. His dark hair curled over his scalp in thick waves. His nose appeared to have been broken at some time. The breadth of his shoulders and the size of his arm muscles couldn't even be covered by the fashionable three-piece suit he was wearing. His face softened into almost a smile. "I must have the wrong door." His hand came out and lightly nipped at my left tit. "Too bad about that."

"You...you could call downstairs to find out what the right room number is if you'd like." Jesus, why did I say that? Because he exuded animal sex, that's why. Because I knew his cock would be enormous and because I still had some of my morning hard-on left.

"You want me to find another room?"

"I don't know what you mean." I thought that answer gave me a minute to think. But he didn't hear a hesitation.

"Sure you do, kid. But don't worry." He went past me into the room. "Close the door and get rid of those pants."

He crossed the room and sat on one of the two big comfortable chairs. I froze. "Look, I've just had some bad experiences, I really don't think you should stay." But something about him came over me. I sensed tremendous power in him. My hands ignored my head and took off the pants.

"You'd be a lot more convincing, kid, if you still had your clothes on. Give me a light."

He had taken out a cigar. I walked over to him and picked up one of the books of matches from the table. I struck a flame and touched it to his cigar. "I mean it, mister. I don't mean to be difficult. But I've had a bad time. I shouldn't have let you in and I shouldn't have taken off my pants. But now, please, will you leave?"

"Kid, you're in the Plaza. You're in a room with a very busy and very important man who just happens to be very horny and very turned on to you. Nothing could possibly happen to you. I have a meeting in the hotel. This meeting is worth millions of dollars to me, but it also just so happens that I want a piece of that nice ass. No one turns me down, kid. Hand me the phone."

I had thought he was vaguely familiar, and now I knew. His picture had appeared in every newspaper in town. A flush of anxiety swept over me as I recognized his face.

I handed him the house phone and watched his handsome features while he puffed on the cigar and got a hold of the operator, getting himself connected to another room where his gruff voice told them, "Tough shit... I'll get there when I can... At least another hour... So buy him breakfast."

He slammed the receiver down. "Asshole." He turned to me. "Kid, don't ever do any business with Krauts. Those Germans are all a pile of shit...more trouble than they're worth."

One of his hands reached out and drew me closer to him. The warmth of his palm spread over my ass. "You're hot, kid. Shaved, too. Who did that?"

"My master."

"Master, huh? Into the SM stuff?" I nodded. "That's okay, kid, don't worry about me. You recognize my mug shot?" I nodded again. "Yeah, I thought you might. They usually do. But I'm not going to hurt you, kid. Come here, sit on my lap." He pulled me still closer and soon I found myself on his thighs; my hairless, bruised skin scratched against the rough wool of his pants. My arms had no place to go except around his neck. One of his own arms came around my waist. "I like little guys like you, kid." One of the wide palms cupped my asscheek. "And with no hair, you look even younger." His tongue came out and started to lick at my pecs, finding my nipples. Their training showed forth again with sighs that came out of me before he expected them. "Feels good, huh, kid?"

"Yes, Sir."

"No, kid, not 'Sir.' *Daddy!* You call me *Daddy*, kid." His hands started a caress of my rump just when the door knock came. "Come in," he yelled out. I started to jump up, but he held me tight. "Don't worry, son, it'll be all right." The same old man as last night came in. How could he still be working? He wordlessly set up the table in the middle of the floor. He came over to the pair of us in the corner when the breakfast was all laid out. "You did good, Jocko. Keep up the good work." The waiter left.

"You see, kid, I got my own little trip going with boys. You have the kind who want you to beat them up. And the kind that want to make love. Me, I just like to take care of my little fellas. Now you, you must be hungry. Come over here." He pushed me gently off his lap and went to the one chair at the table and sat down. He patted his thighs. "Come on, kid."

I was totally lost now. Here I was, all alone in a hotel room with one of the biggest and best-known figures of the Mafia, and he's treating me like a long-lost son. When I climbed back on his lap I was sitting on a different knee. But the lump I felt against his chest did nothing to calm me down. "Daddy" had a gun.

He was massive. I don't think he was as tall as Mr. Benson, but he definitely was more muscular. I thought I remembered that he had been a boxer once. I asked him.

"Yeah, kid. A long time ago. And I kept the old machine in pretty good shape, don't you think?" He slapped his side for emphasis.

He was cutting the breakfast steak I had ordered with a knife. I was shocked when the piece came up to my mouth. "Come on, kid, open up for Daddy." I chewed on the food. I gulped it down, half in fear. "Hey," his voice was suddenly sharp, "Not so fast. You have to chew your food better than that or you'll get a spanking." I had a sudden insight into what was going on. The size of the man and the presence of the gun were all that I needed to stay in line. I took a very, very long time chewing the next piece of steak.

"That's better, son. Now here, take a swallow of milk." He even held the glass for me while I drank. The whole breakfast went down like that. I hadn't been treated that way since I was in kindergarten. When I had eaten everything on the plate he told me I was a good boy. "A very good boy."

This was a trip I don't think even Mr. Benson could have taken me on. I didn't know the cues, and I was more frightened of this man than I had been of the brute the night before. "Come on, time to go potty, son."

Potty?

He led me into the bathroom, pulled down the seat of the toilet and sat on it. He held on to my waist with one arm, and with the other took a large bath towel off the rack. He spread my legs, and then tied the corners of the towel—a diaper! He made a diaper for me out of the towel!

His hands slid up and down my sides. He didn't watch me, but kept his eyes glued to my crotch. "Come on, boy, pee-pee for Daddy. Show Daddy how you pee-pee." I knew what I was supposed to do and strained against my empty bladder, but finally forced down a flow, enough to dampen the thick towel. The piss flowed down from the cotton fabric and on to the floor. "Bad boy!" But he had told me to! "Wetting your diapers. You'll have to have a spanking!"

He tore the towel off me and threw it into a corner. He took a washcloth and soaked it under the sink faucet. "Spread your legs so daddy can clean you off." The warmth bathed my skin gently.

After being alone for a while, almost a whole day now, and after having learned to get into all of Mr. Benson's trips, my mind was ready for almost everything, I guess. I was surprised when I heard myself. "I'm sorry, Daddy, I didn't mean to do it."

A clean, soft, dry towel was rubbing against me now. Why was I responding this way? My cock was hard. Was it just the touch of the warm hands and the soft cloth? Or just having someone to take care of me again? "I won't do it again, Daddy. Please don't spank me."

"Son, you have to learn not to go pee-pee in your diapers. I told you before, didn't I?" A hand slapped out at my bare rump. Tears came to my eyes more copiously and more readily than ever before.

"I won't do it again, Daddy."

"Stop whining." The voice had become harsher. I had to pull back before I took this too far.

He grabbed my wrist and dragged me back into the bedroom. He sat down in the chair again, still holding onto my arm. "Over my lap."

Placidly, I bent over his knees. "Daddy's very sorry to have to do this, son, but you have to learn." And the hand started coming down. I squirmed against the anticipated blows before they fell on my ass, feasting on their touch to the bruises from last night. He stopped suddenly. "Who did this to you?"

I was sniffling. "Some guy last night."

"Did you ask for it?"

"No, Daddy."

"Did you want it?"

"Not...that way."

"Jesus, what a bastard." He was very serious now. "Tell me what happened."

The whole story came flooding out—about my being on my own for a weekend—I didn't tell him all about Mr. Benson—and going to the bar, the guy picking me up, and my waking in the doorway when he was done.

"I'm sorry, son, I didn't really know they were bruises at first, I mean what bad bruises they were. I figured you had just gotten out of a hot bath and had some leftover marks, but Christ, this!" His hand went over the welts that were raised so high I could sense the ridges as his hands passed over them. "To think someone would do this to one of Daddy's boys. Poor little guy." He rolled me over somehow so I was facing up, being supported by his enormous arms. He stood and carried me over to the bed effortlessly.

"Poor little fella, getting beat up like that." He stretched me out on the bed and stood beside it, stripping himself quickly. The torso he revealed had more to do with a gorilla than a man. It was thick with dark hair formed into mounds by the well-developed muscles. The belly was swollen out, but firm to my touch when he lay beside me on the bed and gathered me up into his arms again. A cock that was as wide as my wrist shot out from the hairy growth, pressing against my stomach. His litany never faltered. "Poor kid, let me hold you. Let Daddy make everything feel okay for you."

I responded. Little boy tears came from my eyes as I talked more about the sadist from last night. I stuck my head into the warm neck and told Daddy how frightened I was, how scared, how I had wanted someone to take care of me.

"Daddy's here now, son, Daddy's here." The cock worked its way between my legs and a gentle, slow thrusting began, the cock only grazing my asshole, my own cock rubbing against the warmth of his stomach matting.

His hands each softly cupped one of my cheeks; he held me tight. His body suddenly and luxuriously drenched itself in sweat; the hair clung to his skin revealing more of the heavy muscles. I kept expecting him to fuck me, worrying about the size of his prick forcing its way into me. But he shot right like that, his come squirting behind me. "Daddy's boy, Daddy's boy, Daddy's boy," he moaned as he clutched me to him hard, holding on as much as he could.

My own erection stood out from my stomach, waiting for release. As soon as he regained his breathing, he reached down and grasped it, gently pulling on its length and still keeping one of my cheeks in his other palm. "Come on, boy, shoot your come for Daddy. Come on, let it come out all over Daddy." This strange new chant continued for a few minutes until I felt the pulsing of my prick quicken, the hardness went stiff and the spasms of orgasm pushed through me. My come was added to the heavy-smelling sweat on his body. "Good boy, that's a good boy." He clutched me to him so forcibly I thought I would lose a rib.

We lay there on the bed, just staying quiet for a long five minutes. I enjoyed the feeling of being enveloped by so large a man, of being held after only one night away from Mr. Benson. I kept my face nestled in his neck, softly rubbing against the fur of his body.

"That was wonderful, kid," his words signaling an obvious end. He pulled himself away from me and got up by the bed. "You're a real good boy." A hand came down and patronizingly patted my head. "I don't like people fooling around with good kids like you. You want me to do something about that guy?"

I had a flashing view of the leatherman from last night wearing cement boots and being tossed into the Hudson. It was an intriguing image, but I thought better of saying it out loud. People like this man don't make fine distinctions between fantasies and realities. "No, thank you. It's as much my fault as anything. I was stupid to have gone home with him without knowing what would happen."

"Well, I suppose you're right, but I don't like the idea of people like that creeping around the city." He had become very businesslike again. He went into the bathroom and I thought about the strange but strangely pleasant trip we had just gone on. I thought about what might have happened if he hadn't seen my scars and become so concerned. I pictured myself sitting on his lap and being fed every meal, wearing diapers and wetting my pants. It wasn't a scene to make me want to do it again, but it had been interesting. That was for certain.

He dried himself in the doorway of the bathroom. The thick hair resembled a fur coat again as if fluffed up from the towel. He was really immense. I giggled thinking of this fearsome criminal feeding his "boy" dinner and spanking him for wetting diapers. "You want a doctor or something, kid? I mean for those bruises?"

My own hand went out and ran over the surface of the skin. "No thanks, again. I think it'll be okay. They only hurt if I lean right on them. I don't think there's anything really to be done. He didn't cut me or break anything."

He was pulling on his trousers by now. "OK, but if you ever need anything, anything at all, you just tell that bellhop. He can get a message to me anytime, anytime at all. You understand?" The last sentence was more an order than a sentence.

"Yes, Daddy."

The smile came back as he tied his tie and reached out to pat my head again. "I take care of my little boys; every one of them is special to me."

He finished dressing and walked to the door. Suddenly I thought of something. "Daddy?" He stopped and turned to me. "Daddy, do you know anything about some gay guys who are missing? Did it have anything to do with the guy last night?"

His stare was stern. "I told you not to have anything to do with Krauts, didn't I? Well, stay away from Germans. That's an order."

The door slammed behind him before I could ask anything more.

I found Rocco at the bar that night. The horrible bruises on my body had healed enough to let me walk comfortably, at least. Their dark red marks on my skin were a constant reminder of the safety I had left when I had walked out of Mr. Benson's door. They reminded me of how much I wanted to be back there.

But an afternoon of soaking in a hot tub and eating good food had helped a lot. I was anxious to see Rocco and to find out what was happening with the mystery of the missing men. I was especially anxious that he hear my news.

I was surprised by the almost sad face that greeted me. My friend Rocco, the one who I had shared so much with, almost seemed to try to ignore me. I couldn't figure out why. "Jamie, here, here's a beer. Look, I gotta talk to you, but not now. Not at the bar. Wait for my break, will you? It'll only be another half an hour."

I went over to the other side of the room and pondered the almost put-off way that Rocco was acting. Was something wrong with Mr. Benson? A flash of fear went through my body. I was just beginning to understand how much I needed him. I had begun to think about Mr. Benson as though he were indestructible. But in some ways he was human. Could he have been hurt?

Or did it have to do with the missing men? My

mind went over the little information Rocco and I had. Maybe someone was here in the bar and Rocco didn't want him to know we were aware of the things that were happening. Maybe.

The half hour went by with excruciating slowness. My mind was in a frenzy by the time Rocco came around from behind the bar and joined me with a fresh beer.

"Rocco, what is this? Why are you being so weird?"

"Oh, Jamie, I just don't know how to tell you."

"Tell me what?" It was Mr. Benson! I knew it! I just knew that something had happened to him!

"Jamie, he brought that other guy to the club-house last night," Rocco blurted out. He had a small tear coming down from one of his eyes. I looked at his face without understanding what he had just said.

"Well? So?"

"But, Jamie. He said he was Mr. Benson's new slave. He said he had kicked you out. Did he? Jamie, what happened?"

I felt as though a pile of bricks had dropped on my chest. That was the moment when I understood the true vulnerability of being a slave, the real risk that you take. It all went through my mind in an instant. All the submissions I had made flashed through me. Each one that had been exciting or adventuresome or had been meant to be dedications of myself to Mr. Benson became searing humiliations.

I had shaved my body for this man, this man whose piss I drank, this man who kept me locked up without clothes or freedom for weeks. He had just dumped me. And I was left with nothing but the stripped-away vision of an asshole! Me! A stupid asshole for him to have used. He was telling the truth when he had called me that. It was all I had meant to him.

My face flushed as I thought of the self-deception I had practiced. How could I have been so foolish? Thinking that his taking care of me was part of the same relationship as the degradation I had gone through. Thinking that his true feelings were being expressed in the abuse he had heaped on me.

The brand! Branded on the ass by someone who would so easily throw me away! My hand went down and rubbed against the bruised skin and I realized that the marks from the evil sadist the night before and the scar that Mr. Benson had inflicted on me were the same thing. The same misuse of my body—just two different men who had more in common than not.

An angry tear came out of my eye, but mixed with shame and guilt at what I had gone through.

"What did they do?" The words came out through clenched jaws. The violence in them shocked Rocco.

"Jamie, look, they...they just went through the motions. Maybe they were just joking." He knew his words were lies and the heated stare I gave him made him admit it. "The usual." His voice dropped as he gave up trying to fool me.

"The *usual*!" My fury returned. How could Rocco call what I had been through the *usual*?

"I mean..." he stammered, "Jamie,...he...didn't brand him."

"That's supposed to make me think that it's all okay. Because I *do* have the asshole's brand on me!" My jaws had broken loose from their rigid set and my voice had risen to a scream.

"Jamie, look, calm down..."

"Calm down!" The scream rose again.

"Jamie, not here, not in the bar." He took my arm with one hand and removed the beer bottle with the other. "Come on, let's go for a walk."

He led me out of the bar. The sudden gust of air hit me with a cool force, and the aloneness of a dark street in the Village let loose a wild sobbing from deep in my gut.

Rocco put an arm around me, I guess trying to comfort me, but the move only brought a deeper, angry cry from within me. The humiliation swept over me again. Rocco had seen it all! He had seen what Mr. Benson had done to me. He had seen Mr. Benson take on another slave. I cried into his chest and thought of the enormous shame I had felt. The horror of what I had allowed to be done to me! And to think I had once viewed it as my manhood that I could give to a man like him.

The others went through my mind. Larry, with his fucked-up values, wasn't so off-base, was he? There were no men in gay life who were going to treat anyone with any decency. The sadist last night? He wasn't really any different than Mr. Benson, it seemed now. And the strange gangster. Who could call anyone else strange when he himself had spent a month never sitting on a piece of furniture and polishing someone else's toilet bowl like it was a throne.

God, what a fool I'd been!

The sobs kept heaving, straining my chest muscles with sharp pain. The water from my tears was joined by a flow from my nose and mouth. I had broken down completely. The gulping of my chest and the crying left me weak. Soon Rocco was holding me up. "Oh, Rocco, Rocco, how could you have let me? How could you have let me make such a fool of myself?"

I slid to the ground and he stood there, trying to make soothing sounds to comfort me. Finally, I don't know how much later, it stopped. There were no more tears left.

A sudden sobriety came over me. My job! Suddenly I was left with the dilemma of re-entering the real world. The fantasy of being cared for was gone. But my job! I had given it up. And my apartment! I had no place to live.

Just like any other fairy who was foolish enough to believe in love. A heavy depression sank over me. There was no difference at all between two florists getting together and owning a shop and what I had just put myself through. At least they probably had a legal contract.

I felt the lump of money still in my back pocket. I suddenly understood why he had given me so much. It was to leave for good. Give the little guy a suit of leather and a roll of dough and he'll forget all about it.

I wanted to tear the bills up and throw them down in the gutter. The tight pants and the awkward position were all that stopped me. I collapsed after a weak attempt to pull the money out. Why be foolish? I knew I would really need it. I had no place to go. I couldn't return to my old roommate and let him see the state I had sunk to.

And still more humiliation. Mr. Benson had given me five thousand dollars. At the time I thought it was his generosity. Now I knew it was the price tag he had put on me. Five thousand dollars! Should I consider it salary? A month's work?

I could barely hear Rocco trying to speak to me. "Jamie, I know he didn't throw you out. He wouldn't do that. He just wouldn't, Jamie. There must be a reason for it."

I shook my head sadly. "No, Rocco, that's just what did happen. Did you see that guy?" I lifted my head up to look in his face. My red-streaked face didn't matter to me now. He nodded. "Then you

141

know how beautiful he was. You know who he was, don't you?" Again he nodded. "And look at me, Rocco. I'm just some little queer who thought he had a right to something better in his life. That's my foolishness, Rocco. Do you know, when we had a threeway, all I could think about was how lucky I was to be Mr. Benson's slave and to have a chance, any chance at all, to sleep with someone like that model. I just thought about how fortunate I was to be given the opportunity. Instead, it gets me out on the street. Every detail I think about, Rocco, just adds to the embarrassment."

"What are you going to do, Jamie?"

"What else does a used slave do, Rocco? I'm going to clean up and go find some cock to suck. What else can I do?" The sobs started coming up again. Rocco tried to talk to me, but I could tell by the way he kept glancing at his watch that he was worried about his job. I could barely make out his words through my fog of self-pity and disgrace, but I heard him asking me to come into the bar with him. Somehow, I got up and followed him back around the corner and into the dark space.

I found myself pulling on a good, cold bottle of beer. The sudden chill woke up my throat and my insides. I took another swig and then went up to the bar to get a third bottle. That was three more than I was used to having.

"Hey, Jamie, what you think you're doin'?" Rocco never did lose that concerned look of his. "Getting drunk isn't going to help any."

"Rocco, just give me a beer. Here's the money." I was so concerned with blocking out the pain that I couldn't care less about his feelings. The new beer came across the surface and hit my hand. I grabbed it and downed it, and another, and another—three more in a half hour. Finally, the longed-for haze of alcohol took over my brain and soothed the nerve endings that I had thought would drive me insane. A kind of calmness came over me.

So. I was an asshole. But he was too. What kind of prick is he that he marches around in the skin of a dozen animals and makes like he's some little earth-bound god? He's no better'n me. Him and that pretty boy model of his.

A mound of self-justifications built themselves up in my head.

Master! Master, indeed! His belly's too soft and he doesn't get enough exercise and he listens to too much goddamn classical music! Just another pretentious faggot!

I knew I didn't believe any of it.

EIGHT

A slave has no dignity without a master.

If I ever need proof of that, all I have to do is remember that night when Rocco told me that Mr. Benson had taken a new slave and had kicked me out. I started by drinking too many beers at the bar where Rocco worked. An alcoholic clarity came over me at first. It tried to explain away Mr. Benson and my need for him. It tried to convince me that he was just another trick, nothing to worry about. But that couldn't last long.

Instead, reality took over. I was a slave without a master. I had been stripped of my ability to care for myself in the world and suddenly sent out on the sea without an oar. I had been taught not to make decisions, and now I couldn't even decide where I was going to go. I couldn't stay in the bar and accept Rocco's pitying stares. I had to leave.

I finally left the bar and tried to think of my next move. Where could I go? If a slave is left without control of his life, he is also left with something else: unbridled sexual need. Every single defense that American society puts up against the expression of sexuality is torn away from a slave. He is left wanting—no, needing—his master's cock and now I had only the need without the master.

Everything I was depended on having a man in control of me. Now I had to find a man. I headed for the Mineshaft. As I walked along, the slick surface of my thighs and ballsac rubbed against one another. I felt my skin pucker at my asshole. Until someone has taken it away from you, you never know what your pubic hair is for. It's to protect your cock, balls and ass, sure, but did you know from what? From your own sexual awareness. Taking away that hair and making you sense your sex parts directly is one of the ways a top makes you into a slave, a slave to the needs that only he can fulfill. I thought about that as I walked toward the river. I thought about the smooth mounds rubbing against one another and how it made me aware of the hole in my ass. The hole I needed to get filled by some man. The need I had for a man.

I was frightened. I was scared to be alone now. I thought of Mr. Benson's real sadism: creating this new man and then abandoning it. Leaving me with the defenses down and the vulnerabilities open.

I had never needed sex the way I had after I met Mr. Benson. Oh sure, I always wanted it, but not need. Now my ass cried out for fulfillment. My whole body needed to feel a man's hand against it.

When you're a slave and you give in to the demands of a master, you are someone. But being someone demands having a master to give you meaning. You let them take it from you to give you something better back. That's what Mr. Benson had done to me. I had given him all I had and he had given me back a life and identity that were even better. That's why I had done it, for Chrissakes, to belong to him. But I had left myself open and weak in the process. And now I had nothing.

Nothing but need and desire and fear.

I went up the stairs to the dark bar and paid my money to get in. The leather outfit I had on tonight made it a lot easier than before. Shit. I had forgotten that other time, when Mr. Benson had begun my training by making me wait here for him, standing in a jockstrap stripped for the eyes of all these men, waiting for Mr. Benson to arrive—only to be taken away to the night of my greatest trial. Now I had full leather; no sweat, the doorman doesn't know what's going on in your psyche. He doesn't care what you're here for. He just takes the money and you're inside.

I felt more naked now than I had before. Then I had known Mr. Benson was coming. Then I hadn't had to pay attention to any of these men watching me. I could just stand there and wait. But now...

At first, I looked for someone to take me home and hold me and tell me I'd make it through the night. I looked around, no, I did more than just look—stared down every one of them. I was hot. I knew I was hot. Mr. Benson had told me so. Maybe the man in the flannel shirt would take me home and play forest ranger, and then take me to bed and hold me. I looked over and tried to get a response from his thick-browed eyes. No luck. Was my need too obvious? Was I scaring him?

I tried to relax. Don't scare them with the enormity of your need, I thought, just snare one of them. Any one of them. There was an older man on the pool table. Good-looking guy, maybe 45. Age wasn't important. Hell, I didn't even know how old Mr. Benson was. I tried to catch his glance, but pretty soon it became obvious he couldn't see anyone who wasn't black.

I got another beer. Now I was giving up. I didn't have the strength to go through this bar-cruising game. I was trying to calm the pain inside me, the horrible fear of the loneliness that gripped my stomach. If I can't find a man this way, at least I could find someone to fill the hole in my ass, I thought.

Suddenly my mind was whirling with the space that was there between my legs. The void that I had never even known about until Mr. Benson had shown me it was there and that I had needed him to fill it. I walked into the backroom.

The group of men in the dim light walked around the vertical beams, the ones that showed where the stairs were to go down into the basement of horrors. The same beams that held up the black leather sling, swinging between the supports with the softest of spotlights on it, illuminating the pouch of the leather so slightly you would hardly notice if it weren't for the surrounding total darkness.

I walked over and leaned against one of the supports. I waited to see who was playing the game tonight. Who could help me fill this emptiness inside me?

There were others like me—the ones who wanted to be hunted. They circled with different degrees of overtness, opening themselves up to the attacks of the men they hoped would be hunters.

I never understood the game that much. I had never understood the difference between being open and waiting for Mr. Benson to choose when to swoop down and that of being there and waiting to see who might swoop down. To know it might be Mr. Benson didn't detract from my dignity. I was owned. There was pride in that ownership. To be vulnerable to Mr. Benson meant to be vulnerable to the man who owned me. But there is no dignity to a slave without a master. To be that open was to be degraded. I saw it in the faces and actions of the men who circled the sling, waiting to be put in it and to have their needs met by a stranger without care and without pride. Mr. Benson had taken away my pride, but then he had replaced it with a new kind—the pride of belonging.

But now I was like the rest of them: in such great need that anyone who would pay attention would be the man for tonight. There was no emotional bond to be considered. What had to be considered was the total lack of pride. It dawned on me that I was there as an object who could be given meaning only if someone found it attractive. There was nothing attractive about me until a man placed value on it. That was what it meant for me to have become a slave. To place myself in the position that the other person had to value me. I was devastated now because that other person had found me worthless. But I had given up my self-worth! And now I needed a man to find me in this place and show me that it was worthwhile to live again. I was no longer different the way I had been when I was with Mr. Benson. I had taken the risk for the chance to get something more. And I had lost.

My mind took all that in as it watched the endless parade. There were ten others who were like me, I decided. Their need was even more obvious, though, in their clothes or lack of them. The man with the seat of his pants torn off with the Crisco seal on his belt buckle; he left nothing to the imagination. Nor did the other guy who wore only a jockstrap, a pair of heavy black boots and a red handkerchief around his neck. In every intermediate state of undress were the others, walking around the sling, trying not to be so obvious about what they wanted from one of the black knights who slink around the walls, watching them the way hawks watch pigeons in the park. Sitting ducks, any of them, any one of *us*, ready for their attack.

I was being too coy. One of the older men gave up

the game. He wasn't going to play anymore. I gave him that, I gave him some measure of dignity. I stood there, leaning against the post, but he just finally up and got into the sling all by himself.

He sat back in it and hooked his legs around the chains coming down to hold up the pouch. He took a paper cup of Crisco—the kind they give you in the bar—and he greased his ass, exposing it to the stares of the crowd. The on-lookers came in, those "watchers" from Jersey and Long Island who don't know how to play this game that fascinates them so. They crowded around him. A couple started to touch him, feel him up. If they were attractive and knew their place he let them, but most he pushed away. When you play this game, you know who's on the team opposing you and who's supposed to sit in the bleachers.

There was something about this guy admitting it, I thought. At least he puts it on another level. But to spread his legs to God and man that way, it was not like doing it for Mr. Benson. There was no dignity in spreading it—your open asshole—to the world. The dignity was being able to spread it to the man that owned it.

The guy pulled a huge dick out of the shorts he was wearing and started to beat off, trying to lure one of the hunters away from their perches along the dark wall, where we all knew they were. It only attracted more attention from the Tunnel and Bridge people—those men who live half-lives in garden suburbs and travel over bridges and through tunnels only at night to taste the life that the rest of us choose to drown in. The hunters didn't move. There was no good reason to be there, in the sling, getting a blow job from someone you knew wore polyester six days a week. The guy got disgusted and shoved away the tourists who were feeling his hard muscled body. He got up, disgraced, and stood back in the line of the men circling the sling.

At least he had tried. I still stood, wearing the black leather that didn't define me, leaning against the post. The leather made them all wonder. I was not in the hunters' section, where leather was dominant. But I didn't circle either. I wasn't committing myself. There was no dignity to being a slave without a master, but there was tremendous need.

I didn't have the luxury of not trying, I thought to myself. I stood forward into the glow of light around the sling. The circle stopped moving. It meant a performer was going to make his move. They knew it and they waited for me to commit myself to my role. The Tunnel and Bridge people gawked; they only knew it was leather. A black knight, they probably all thought, and they moved toward me. But I pushed them away. The rest of the players in the macabre dance knew. I hadn't told anyone my character yet. They all waited.

I took off the heavy jacket and laid it over the railing of the stair. It was a very stupid thing to do with something that cost hundreds of dollars. But I was in no mood for security. I was in need. I struggled to get out of my boots without bending over. I was trying valiantly to keep from having to have to kneel in this light in front of all these people. One by one, the boots came off. Then, as slowly as I dared, and about as fast as I could given how much I had drunk, I undid my belt and peeled off the leather pants.

The breathing in the room was faster; you could feel it. I was young, and well built, and hot. No one, not even Mr. Benson in his absence, could take that from me. The hard body I now showed them was almost totally shorn of hair. My nudity excited the men who knew how to play the game; it shocked the rest. Listening to their quicker tempo of breath, I climbed up onto the platform the other man had left and sat on the cool pouch, its surface only slightly warmed by the body that had left it. I lifted up my bare legs and leaned back into the sling. Waiting to see if a hunter would come out from the shadows to take me.

The cool air circulated around my nude asshole. The gaping anus seemed to cry out in a voice all of its own. The need to be filled. Come on, assholes, fill it up! Don't let this void go empty any longer.

A blackness came from the shadows, more quickly than I had expected. It loomed over me, a white face revealing itself from the folds of black leather and night. A jacket was removed. The sudden appearance of massive, white arms startled me and the crowd. The circling had stopped completely. The people moved into the center, not around it. A silence came over us all. And only the beat of loud music filled the air. Even the Tunnel and Bridge people knew that "something" was happening. There was a heaviness in the look the man gave me. Hard, cold, stern. My response was just as solid.

The star players had taken their characters. Somehow a cup of Crisco came into his hand. He took some of the white goo, spreading it over his forearm and down over his fist. He took another handful and rubbed the lubricant over his fingers. All the time he stared right into me, but beyond me. He didn't know who I was, and I didn't care. He was greasing up an arm that'd spent plenty of time in a gymnasium: A thick, hairy arm that was going to silence the screaming need of my ass, of my bowels, of myself, if only for a few minutes.

The slippery hand came down and touched my ass;

the fingers slid into my crack. I threw back my head. I didn't want to watch anymore. I wanted to be full. I wanted that hand inside my ass, filling me up the way I had gotten used to. My arms went out and grabbed the back set of chains. A vial of amyl came out of the darkness and filled my head. The hand pushed against my sphincter. Then...suddenly...painfully...too quickly...he was inside me, grasping inside me. Pulling. Pushing. Shoving. Ignoring my moans and loud cries. I felt mouths come down on my tits—warm, moist lips covering each of them. Someone went down on my cock and rode it in unison with his fist. Was it him? I couldn't see. I could only feel. And more amyl came to my face. I was full and warm with his fist and those mouths and those hands running over the exposed parts of my body.

For one split second I was filled up and covered and taken care of. For one split second I could feel all right. Then I thought of Mr. Benson and I realized that it wasn't his fist and I cried out—stopping the amyl from coming to my face again and pushing against the fist in my ass—trying to get rid of these foreign objects entering me. *They weren't Mr. Benson!*

They ignored me. They took it all for passion, or release, or something. I soon collapsed against the strain of bodies rubbing and pushing through me. I let them take their pleasure and their want and leave me, one by one. Their dramatics didn't affect me any more. The pacing was up to them. The applause I would receive for this performance wasn't enough to make up for losing Mr. Benson.

Soon enough it was over. I was left panting in the sling. They stood around, the tourists in awe, the hunted in jealousy, the rest of the hunters wondering if they wanted a part of the action. My own hunter was in front of me, between my outstretched legs, wiping his greasy arm with a paper towel, a smile of satisfaction on his face. He had scored. He was proud of himself. But he wasn't my master, and his score meant nothing to me. It gave me no dignity.

They begrudgingly let me recover. As soon as I could, I climbed down out of the sling and collected my clothes. I went into a corner and struggled with them. Finally I gave up and just put on my boots. I had tucked the money into my soles and, by then now drunkenly, carried the rest to the coatcheck.

Somehow, ridiculously, I had kept my cap on through the whole thing. Now my disappointment and drinking had left me without an iota of concern for the dignity I could not have without my master. I walked back into the rear of the Mineshaft in just that leather motorcycle hat and my boots. Naked, shorn of hair, without anything more than what I had to offer: A body.

I was no longer even in need. There was no need. There couldn't be any success in my quest. Mr. Bensons find you when you don't expect them. That's a part of who they are, I thought. Mr. Benson wouldn't come to the Mineshaft looking for a slave; he'd find one on the street or in a Christopher Street bar or—goddamn it—in a magazine ad, just like the new slave Mr. Benson had found. And what was going to happen to that guy? I wondered. What would happen to him? He might be the face that means "cigarettes" to half of America, it wouldn't make any difference. After what I had been through, I knew that even he would end up in a place like this, looking for any symbol that would help him try to take away the pain.

That searing pain led me to the back bar for still another beer, one that I could hardly say the words to order. I was drowning in the booze and self-pity then. What did I want now? I thought. What could help me now? Proof! It came over me. Proof that I wasn't worthwhile, that I wasn't a person that counted. I needed proof, still, that Mr. Benson was right. I was a slave. I was to be used. That was all I knew anymore. And I hadn't anything that would save me from the fate. There was no master who valued me enough to make it all right.

Mr. Benson was right about some things, still, I had to admit. I was a toilet. Any one of these guys had a right to use an asshole/slave/cocksucker like me for a toilet. I half walked, half fell down the stairs to the darkness of the bottom floor of the Mineshaft, into the red light of the piss room. Declarations in a place like this aren't made with words. You don't need words to know that someone is an asswipe/prick/piss-drinker. They let you know. As drunk as I was, I made my declaration.

The tub was in the middle of the room. It was empty for a change. There are actually two here at the Mineshaft. One, though, is subtle, in the dark corner. You can take someone there and it can be between the two of you. There's another one in the middle of the room, right under the red light bulb, where you let them know how much you love piss. If that's what is true. If you love piss. Or you show them what you'll do for your master, how you'll climb into a bathtub full of piss if he wants you to. If you have a master. Or you can show them what you think of yourself. Like I did just then, right away. You can climb in over the rim of the tub and lie there, exposed to all of them—you don't care who—and have them fling their fat cocks over the side and let loose a flow of hot piss all over you, 'cause that's what you are, that's what your man taught you.

You're a piss slave, someone who doesn't deserve anything but their waste coming over your body.

That's what I did that night. I lay in the tub with my mouth open, without a hard-on, without any pleasure, waiting for the whole group of them to come over and unload on me, waiting for them to confirm what I knew I was, a piss slave, a shithead/asshole-eating slave who didn't even have a master. Just someone for each of them to use as a urinal.

I was almost oblivious to the stench as each one of them came over to the tub and pulled out his dick—thick, skinny, cut, uncut, black, white, brown, fat, lean, beautiful, ugly. I never looked at their faces, I just took their piss. Drenched myself in their golden shower. Tried to drown myself in their abuse.

All I could think about was Mr. Benson's piss. The beautiful flow of gold that came out of his cock and went down my throat every day. I thought of Mr. Benson's perfect uncut cock slipping down my throat, making my mouth a better place with the discharge of his sweet urine.

I finally climbed out. The liquid poured off my body. I shrugged off the people who wanted to drag me into a corner. The ones who thought they had a right to the use of this urinal. There were no Mr. Bensons there. I staggered into the furthest room of the bar, where there was more beer. I dragged, somehow, a dollar out of my boot and took a long pull out of the bottle of cold liquid, hoping it would flush down some of the bitter taste that stayed in my throat. Now the alcohol wasn't diminishing the pain anymore. It was letting it flow. I had to feel something besides this emptiness. I had to think of something besides Mr. Benson.

I looked around the room; the figures were beginning to blur in my vision. The real black knights were there, lining this inner sanctum of the place, waiting for the ones who could really take it here in this, the best-lit room, the room without the protection of darkness. I thought to myself: come and get it, come and get your piece of meat, take what you want, how you want, anything any of you want, it's yours.

One of them moved into the brightest lights and the beer didn't stop me from seeing that he was looking at me. Nor did it stop me from noticing the belt that he carried: heavy black leather. The strap was looped around his fist; only the buckled end was hanging down. The color faded into the rest of his outfit of darkness. The stare brought back a pseudo-sobriety again.

I pulled myself up to him. He spread his legs in response. The signals were unavoidable, even to me, even with all that beer, even with the thought of Mr. Benson on my mind. I remembered the pain in my mind and thought I saw a release from it. Here, in the leather in the man's hand, I could escape the pain of Mr. Benson.

I stood and carefully, slowly walked by him over to the stage erected on the other side of the room. I stooped my naked, wet body over the end of the stage and spread apart my ass, waiting for release in the pain.

I knew what was coming. I knew that soon, soon, I would be able to forget Mr. Benson. I knew that the man would see the marks that were still left from the cruel sadist of the other night, and he would misread my desire—or would he? Didn't I want this man and the belt? Didn't I want the marks that would tell me and the rest of the world that I liked to be punished?

I lifted my ass even higher, just as the first blow came down on the tender flesh.

"Hold him." The order went to people I couldn't see. I didn't resist as the hands pulled out my arms and spread my back to the rain of blows that started to fall. There was no tenderness in that beating. It wasn't like when Mr. Benson would beat me. The leather just came down, again and again, savagely striking at my back, my ass, my thighs, my legs, adding to the welts that were there. Warming the surface of my body from my neck to my ankles. And finally, alleviating the pain, taking away my thoughts of Mr. Benson and my failure with welcome waves of sensation over my body.

When he did stop, I realized I had never yelled. Even though the heat of his blows remained after he had ceased the actual beating, I had never called out. When Mr. Benson hit me I kept quiet to prove my manhood to him. That wasn't the case now. I didn't care what these men thought. I suddenly realized what it was that they did think, though; they were frightened! They were frightened!

I stood up painfully and saw the eyes that had witnessed my punishment. They had never seen anything like that. They were in amazement at what I had taken. At first I was going to make like I was proud. Fuckers, I thought, I'll show you. But as soon as I rose to my full height, I fell, collapsing right into the waiting arms of Rocco.

The heat swept over my back as I sat beside Rocco at the bar. He had taken me home that night and somehow had taken care of my skin, torn, but not torn through enough to bleed, by the violent beating. I didn't know how he had gotten me out of the bar and into the cab, let alone how he had dressed me, but the next morning I woke up in his bed, beside him, my head swollen with dehydrating agony from the

158

hangover of my life, the whole of my backside raw from the misuse. I moaned out loud, way out loud. He stirred and sat up in the bed, looking at me through disgusted sleepy eyes. "What kind of fool are you, doing all that to yourself? Do you know what you look like?" I moaned in agony. "Do you know what you smell like?" Another, louder sound came out of my body.

The whole day had been spent trying to care for my hangover. It was, without a doubt, one of the great ones of the century. It was all abetted by the horrible pain that my body had to go through. The welts that rose angry and red from my body, the soreness from my asshole having been stretched to its limits. It was all too much to bear. At least it kept my mind off Mr. Benson.

I was lucky that Rocco was a bartender and had some ideas about how to care for all this. I had hot baths to get steam inside my dried out system, vile tasting liquids to start blood flowing, and salves to calm the screams from the surface of my back. It all took hours. Now we were sitting in a bar together, me at least semi-conscious, taking the last of his cure—a Bloody Mary.

It was already eight in the evening. I sat passively beside him listening to him going on and on and on about what he had gone through to find me. Searching the bars and the baths. "I even would have called Mr. Benson if I could have, but there was a party at the club last night. That's why I didn't have to stay with Brendan. He didn't want me to go. Probably something just for the Topmen."

Even now my acknowledgment was only a moan.

"Have another drink, Jamie. You're going to feel bad tomorrow, too, but you're so hungover it probably won't hurt."

I swallowed another of the red-hot drinks, feeling it burn its way through the mucus that had been collecting in my throat, miraculously after the dryness that had been there.

"Why did you do this to yourself, Jamie? Why?"

"Why not? I'm alone. He took away all my protective covering, Rocco. What am I supposed to do?" I know my voice sounded plaintive. "Am I supposed to go out and find a wife and kids with a brand on my ass?" A tear came down my cheek again, dammit!

We hadn't really talked yet. The whole day had been spent trying to get me in some semblance of shape to face the world. And there was nowhere for this conversation to go. Nowhere but down.

I had avoided it, and now tried to avoid it again by drinking the crimson liquid in front of me and signaling the bartender for another.

"Jamie, that won't do any good, drinking them like that."

"Why the hell not?" It was a bitter voice that answered Rocco that night.

"Jamie, look, it's got to be a mistake. Someone like Mr. Benson doesn't do things like that to his slave. There's a reason, Jamie, I know, and the reason has to do with those men that are missing."

"I don't care about anyone who's missing, Rocco. I just care about me and what the hell I'm supposed to do without Mr. Benson." The last drink went down with a single gulp, and again I was reaching for the bartender.

"Please, Jamie, don't start again. This is enough."

"No, it's not, Rocco." I grabbed a new drink.

An hour later, Rocco and I were both a little smashed as we left the bar and started a familiar trek to the river. It was a weekday. The only place to go this early was the Ramrod. We weaved slightly, but, I thought then, pleasantly as we walked. Rocco had decided not to abandon me and had made a strategic mistake in trying to match me drink for drink. The booze only alleviated my pain and my hangover. It acted more quickly on me, but less dramatically, and I found myself in the funny and difficult position of holding *him* up.

Even with the whole back side of my body burning and with him leaning heavily against me, we looked like a happy pair as we made our way through the Village. We were joking. It felt good, finally to joke and laugh, to be with a friend. It made me feel a little better about the whole, horrible mess I was in. We made eyes at black leather knights as they walked past us, and spent a much too obviously long time staring in the window of a boot shop at West 4th Street, watching the leather-clad salesman trying to make a sale to a man who wore New Jersey on his chest like a neon sign.

We got to Christopher Street and started the descent toward the river by stopping at every bar on the route. Having "just one more," we said to each other. By the time we hit the Badlands at the foot of the street, we were awash in the comradeship of beer. Somehow full of hope, we had gotten to the Ramrod and stood there amongst the early crowd, pleased with ourselves, and me pleased with the world, if only because my friend was with me and I was too drunk to care about Mr. Benson.

We left the Ramrod and decided to walk up the river back to the Eagle and the Spike. It was still absurdly early, but we didn't care. Our arms slung around each other, we weaved up the avenue, singing songs from high school. With Rocco beside me, I was finally out of trouble, I thought. My mind could take a rest. I could deal with living. After Fourteenth

Street, Rocco said he was horny. I didn't know what to do. We couldn't go to the Mineshaft that early. It was still only about ten. Across the avenue were the piers. Drunkenly I told Rocco, "That's what we should do."

"Jamie, Brendan said only fools go to the piers," Rocco slurred. "Brendan said only fools go there who have money to burn and lives to lose."

"Rocco, don't be silly," my own voice answered. "Brendan's being an old lady. Just like *all* the cops. You find something that's fun and a cop will tell you it's a bad thing to do."

We crossed against the traffic and walked up to the entrance to one of the deserted wharves. The glories of New York's days as a worldwide harbor were memorialized by the shell of the wharf that sagged into the river, holding out hope now, not of travel to foreign shores, but of release for Rocco's new-found horniness.

We walked into the darkness and stood straight up, each of us reacting to a primeval call of the wild. Our male bodies knew that there was sex here. Through our drunkenness—dulling my pain and Rocco's sense—all we could hear were the slurping sounds of men meeting each other coming across the vast space of the abandoned sheds. We trod across the area and into the dark closetlike rooms to the source of the sounds, knowing we would find there the release of the physical needs we had. Me for a cock to suck, Rocco for a mouth for his own cock, less trained than mine.

I went first and stumbled over the doorway, falling down onto the ground, right in front of a pair of highly polished boots. They looked familiar. Even through all the Bloody Marys and beer I recognized them. They were just like Mr. Benson's! My head shot up to see if it was him, and instead found the blond, cruel face of Hans. It laughed down at me, talking to someone I couldn't see. Rocco fell over me as the Germanic voice boomed out, "Well, well, it looks like we have just caught two of the best."

NINE

When I woke the next morning, the headache pounding inside me surpassed even yesterday's hangover. I instinctively rubbed my skull and found an egg-shaped lump sticking up through my short hair. I winced at the sharp pain my touch produced, but quickly forgot it when I rolled over on my backside and pressed the floor against the mass of welts that crisscrossed my body with a tender soreness.

Rocco slept beside me. I tried to remember what had happened. How did we end up here, naked? I flashed on Hans's cruel smile bearing down in me, the shiny boots that had reminded me again of Mr. Benson. An electric wave of fear shot through me as I realized that danger was here. I stood up and quickly looked around. We were trapped in a cage. I went over to the steel bars that formed one wall and saw that ours was one of a series of barred rooms on a corridor that looked like the movie set for a cell-block. I went back and shook Rocco out of his sleep. He woke slowly, rubbing his head in a pantomime of my own earlier actions. "Rocco, Rocco, wake up."

He answered with a deep moan. "What the fuck…"

"They've got us, Rocco, they captured us."

"Huh?" He looked around. I could almost see the previous night's activities go through his mind. "Jamie." His voice had a sudden ring of understanding to it. "The murders? Hans?"

"It must be, Rocco, look." I excitedly dragged him up to his feet and pulled him over to the open wall that faced the corridor. Through the other cell doors we could see more naked male bodies, all asleep, it seemed. "It's just dawn," I said, pointing to the very faint light coming from the few small windows. "They're still sleeping."

"But what does it mean, Jamie? What are we here for?"

Almost in answer to his question, a heavy door opened and Hans, in full uniform, the Nazi patch on his sleeve catching the dim dawn with ominous clarity, walked in. A baton in his hand slapped against the steel bars of each cage as he made his way up the line until he was standing directly in front of ours.

"And well, my lovelies, how did you sleep?" He had a monocle in his eye, a caricature of his self-created image.

"What are you doing to us?" Rocco called out. "Why are we here?"

"You are here to fulfill your fondest and finest fantasies, you upstart twerp!" The baton hit the bars and made Rocco jump back a step. "You are here to be sold into slavery."

Hans turned to face his companion, a mean-looking guy who could have fit Central Casting's definition of a hood. "This one will have to be dealt with very strictly. He had ideas that he's not really one of them. He occasionally thinks he is just playing sex games with the dingo lover of his.

"But the other"—he gestured to me—"is the real

thing. A born slave who will draw the highest price, I have no doubt."

They stared into our small arena. "The marks are unfortunate," Hans continued, pointing to the painful stripes on my body. "He obviously found trouble when that pretentious master of his kicked him out." I snarled at the mention of Mr. Benson coming from this asshole's lips. "He cannot be physically punished; we must try to..." He sneered, "...clear up his complexion in time for the sale."

The two of them walked away then, leaving us to listen to the sounds of the waking noises of the other inmates. "Rocco, we're in for it."

The others came to. They were obviously more used to the regimen of the place, and they were waiting for the food that was brought in by Hans's companion and a crony who was pushing a cart of something that produced great clouds of steam.

"On your knees by the bars, assholes," the ugly voice boomed out. "Open your yaps for food."

We watched silently, unbelievingly, as the pair made their way up the line of doors. At each a man, naked as we were, each more beautiful than the next, would kneel at the gate and open his mouth. The terrible-looking keeper would produce his enormous dick, sloppily circumcised by an inept surgeon, and force the captive to suck on its huge width. Only when each had done that did he get a plate of the steaming gruel that was carried on the cart.

They were all fair skinned. Most were blond. Their bodies were universally beautiful. Each of them—I counted twenty-four including ourselves—looked like an advertisement for the all-American boy. Only Rocco's tattoos and my shaved crotch and chest made this seem anything less than the perfect group of

American college students. Midwestern American college students at that.

Finally, they arrived in front of our cage. "On your knees." The order was gruff and matter-of-fact. We didn't move. "You don't understand English? I said on your knees." The keeper's voice was raised; his heavy cock was waving in the air in front of us. "You don't get on your knees, you're getting the beating of your life."

"Hans told you not to harm me. I heard him." I was suddenly grateful for the scars of my backside.

The giant in front of me leered. "But he didn't say anything about your friend there, did he?" He produced a riding crop and it whooshed through the air, banging hard on the metal pole of the bar. "You don't suck my cock, big boy, and your friend here is going to taste leather like he never knew it tasted." The idea appealed to him obviously too much.

I thought quickly. I could—possibly—take more misuse, but not Rocco. He wasn't experienced in the ways of these animals the way that Mr. Benson and my recent adventures had made me. I sank to my knees in front of his foul-smelling prick, ignoring Rocco's pleas. "Don't, Jamie."

But I took it in, almost heaving at the stench rising from the unwashed crotch. "You assholes all gotta learn to suck any time you're told," growled the keeper.

Mercifully, he pulled away his cock and shoved a plastic dish under the cell door. "And you..." He looked at Rocco, offering his cock to my friend. "Suck it." Rocco looked; he hesitated. "Rocco, you need the food. Don't do anything foolish now."

Rocco, his tattooed ass undulating with those hard muscled flanks of his, dropped down and swallowed the unsightly dick.

The keeper was pleased with himself. "You suck cock to eat here. You don't, you don't eat, and you"—he ran the tip of the crop over Rocco's quivering back—"get leather if either you or him give me any trouble." The voice went harsh again after the misleading calm of the orders. "I want no trouble from the two of you from now until the end of the week when I can get rid of you guys."

My mind snapped to attention. The end of the week! Then we'd be free! We watched them walk back down the row of defeated men who silently ate the thick gruel with their hands. Rocco made a face at the mess in the plate in front of him and started to throw it. "No, Rocco, something tells me we might need the energy later. Eat it."

We forced the slop down our throats. When we were done I went over to the wall and made a sound, asking for a response from the next inmate. Each cell was open only on the side facing the hall; the other three walls seemed to be made of concrete. "Hsss." I tried to get an answer. "Hsss."

"Don't, they can hear you outside," a voice finally whispered.

"I'll be quiet. How long have you been here?"

"A month. A month of hell. I'm scared shitless in this place. I've been fucked every day since I have been here."

"Fucked?"

"Yeah, they say they're stretching us. You'll see, later they bring around these dildo-like things and shove them up your ass. They say our masters expect it to be easy to fuck us. Man, I'm stretched further than the Grand Canyon now. Do you know anything about what's going on?"

"Not really, just that a lot of men have been missing, and that they're all attractive."

"Well, they tell us we're here to get new *masters.*" The voice was insolent and I nearly said something, but decided this wasn't the time. "Shit, man, I've never had no *master* at all. A month ago, I just went out and thought I'd be a good lay, ya know? So I went to a leather bar, ya know? The next thing I know this hot dude's hitting up on me and I think I'm going to go to nigger heaven. I go out to his van with him. And then...I wake up in this place sucking smelly cock and eating dirty assholes, getting dildos the size of your arm shoved up me and being told I'm going to be fucking *sold*!"

They were white slavers. I suddenly realized that that must be the trip! That's why so many blonds, only fair-haired guys, only the ones who were so good looking.

A voice had come softly from across the way and made a statement that must have been obvious to our neighbor.

"Have you ever seen such a dick before? Biggest, prettiest cock I ever hoped to suck on."

"How did they get you here?" I broke in before their rhapsody went too far.

"This guy, he takes you into his van and he gets you all hot and undressed. Then he lets you swing on this cock of his. It's huge, just huge and pretty and you don't know what to do with it. Well, anyway," the voice from across the hall tried to recapture himself, "he talks you into letting him fuck you, right there in the back of the van. He tells you he wants you to sit on it..."

"This happened to almost all of us," my neighbor explained.

"Yeah, well," the guy across from us went on, "you get up and squat down on that big fat cock of his and you start pumping away, and just when you know he's going to come, just at that moment when you're ready to give it your all and you're there pumping away at yourself, someone from somewhere comes out of the blue and knocks you cold."

"We figured there was someone hiding up front of the van," the neighbor's voice added.

"That's how most of us came here. Some, this German guy picked them up in the piers or the bushes. Most of us got picked up at bars."

We never could see the neighbor, except glimpses of him, because of the concrete wall. The man across the way, though, was easy to spot. He looked young, I'd say about my age. His chest was covered with that wiry, curly body hair that blonds have. It was thickly matted over his upper torso. They had picked a winner with him, that's for sure. The best part of him was his ass. It was like Rocco's, the kind of ass that has muscles as well developed as a weightlifter's arms. I momentarily wandered into thinking about him and that backside as he stood and walked away from the cell door. I couldn't help but wonder what it would taste like to put my face right up there into the crack between those solid, hard mounds.

Rocco pulled me back to reality. "Jamie, what the hell are we going to do?"

"There's nothing we can do, Rocco, nothing at all. We're trapped here like the rest of them. All we can do is wait."

"We have to get in touch with Brendan, Jamie. He'll get us out."

"And how are we going to do that, send smoke signals?"

The idea caught our minds and we quickly communicated the thought. We looked around the room and groaned. The only furniture was a foam mat we slept on. There was a seatless toilet bowl, just like in

171

a real jail cell. That was all. The floors were covered with linoleum. There was nothing to burn even if we could light it.

"What, Jamie? What are we going to do?"

Our answer was a loud slamming of the door. All the bodies in the row of cubicles rose to go to investigate the strange sounds. Hans and the sadistic jailer both walked in, dragging a body between them. Another captive. Another blond. He was carried/pulled in front of our cell. "Back, assholes," the jailer growled ferociously. We jumped against the far wall as Hans and the other man opened the barred gate and threw the new man into our room.

"A very good specimen," Hans sneered once the weight was relieved. There, right in front of us, sprawled the model, Mr. Benson's new slave!

My first thought was, "Poor Mr. Benson has lost both of us." My second was, "What's that asshole doing here?"

Rocco had run up to the prone body and had cradled it in his arms. He gently slapped the face, trying to bring to consciousness the image that had driven millions of Americans to lung cancer. "Jamie!" Rocco ordered more forcibly when I stood fast.

"Rocco, I don't want to help him." I pointed an accusing finger at the motionless body.

"Jamie, this is not time for your antics. Now get some water." Rocco wasn't buying my act, I guess, and after a minute I did go over and cupped some cold water in my joined hands, carrying it back over to the two of them. I let it run out of my palms, over his face. I enjoyed the sudden splash it made and the way he had to almost throw up to keep from gagging.

"Jamie!" Rocco said accusingly.

"Well, you said..."

By then the model was sitting up, the gleaming

torso outlined by the moisture of sweat and water. The perfect muscles were stark in their relief. The light played with his body as complimentarily as the cameras that had made it famous. I hated him.

He had stolen Mr. Benson from me.

His head protested the pain with an undistinguishable sound. He rubbed his own lump, just as Rocco and I had ours earlier. "Where am I?"

"You're sure as hell not on Fifth Avenue," I spit out.

He turned quickly to face me and blushed, as well he might, when he saw me looking at him. "You."

He moaned again and shakily stood up and looked at me. "How did you get here? You were supposed to be sent away."

"Don't I know it!" I screamed my response.

He looked at me, not understanding the anger in my tone.

"Didn't Mr. Benson send you away?"

"You know he did." My voice almost broke as I screamed at him. "You know he did. He sent me away to take up with you. He kicked me out. He turned me over for"—my look was savage—"*you!*"

"That's not true," he defended himself.

"Man, I saw you," Rocco softly interjected.

"But," the man tried to explain, "that was a set-up, a trick being played on these guys."

Rocco looked as puzzled as I felt. "What do you mean by that?" I finally asked.

"It was a ploy," he whispered, "to get me captured by the ring. I'm supposed to be investigating the disappearances. You two were supposed to be safely put away. What are you doing here?"

"Why you?" I challenged.

"I'm a cop. Undercover. It was set up for me to be captured because Mr. Benson and Brendan didn't want you harmed."

A tear came to my eye. "You mean, you're not Mr. Benson's new slave?"

"I'm a top," he said indignantly.

That I didn't believe. "You sucked *my* cock," I exclaimed.

"That"—he blushed—"that was a test. To see if I could pull off acting like a bottom. Just a test." His voice dropped and he looked away.

"Pretty convincing if you ask me," I pressed. "You sure knew how to follow orders."

His face went even more scarlet. "Yeah, well," he stammered. "Look, that's not the point." He regained his self-control. "The point is, you two are supposed to be safe. Mr. Benson and Brendan wanted you carefully put away just so this wouldn't happen. What the hell am I supposed to do now?"

"What were you going to do in the first place?"

His look made it obvious he was debating answering Rocco's question. He made his mind up. "I'm wired for radio. There's a transmitter in my body. When I activate it, they'll be able to trace me down. They know I'm somewhere in the city."

"Where is it?" I was curious.

He blushed again. "Just you never mind."

Suddenly our conversation was shut off by the loud sound of the cell block door. Hans walked through, followed by the sadist and his helper, and behind them the man who simply must have been the one the others were talking about. The model standing beside me went stiff with recognition. "Jesus Christ" escaped softly from his lips.

If the model was the perfect, living example of America's dream of a fair-haired, blond specimen, the man who strutted down the walk with Hans was its equivalent dream of dark beauty. He was wearing only a pair of Levi's. The eyes that lined the walk were glued to him, and I suddenly realized that even if he was what had lured them to this horrible fate, every one of them thought he was still the most perfect man they had seen.

They weren't that far from wrong. He had a flawless body, just like the model's, and it was covered by a sculptured coating of black body hair. The trail of the dark fur led down into the Levi's that bulged promisingly in the crotch. His white teeth were awesomely bright in contrast to the face, whose rough texture promised the presence of a thick, manly beard.

The foursome stopped in front of our cell. "Well," said Hans, "I told you so."

"Yes, it certainly is him, isn't it?" The new man smiled through a bushy mustache. I had seen him. Him. Of all people! The second-most-famous cigarette model in the country. The one sending as many people off to the shores of Turkey as my unwelcome companion sent off to the ranges of the West.

Rocco and I exchanged blank expressions. It was incredible, but it was true. Here in front of us stood the two most well-known male models in America, the blond cowboy and the dark exotic. They stood facing one another. The blond glared; the other smiled softly.

"This has turned out to be a very advantageous contract, Herr Klaus," the dark man said to Hans with a vaguely foreign accent. "Very advantageous, indeed."

"Yes, Abdul, now you'll be able to control the whole thing yourself, won't you? You can get both contracts."

"Both." He said the words slowly. "But how did you capture him?"

"It was quite interesting, actually." Hans started to explain. "After I rounded up these two"—he pointed at us—"I became intrigued. Why were they on the loose? Mr. Benson, my colleague"—I grated at the way he said that—"is not one to let his slave—the one with the marks—go around free in the city. In fact, I'm sure he's been kept at home for weeks at a time. His presence on the wharf made me think that perhaps there would be something interesting to see at the clubhouse.

"I went down there to check it out. You can imagine my surprise when I found this handsome specimen bound and gagged at Mr. Benson's feet." Hans's crop came out and flicked the blond model's tit. "I had to wait to see what developed. And that was his expulsion." Hans laughed. "Mr. Benson undid the gag and loosened the restraints at one time and this one attempted to tell the famous Mr. Benson off!

"We were all quite incredulous. Even the stupid members of the club don't say to Mr. Benson what this fool said. And, of course, he was immediately thrown out. I could hardly let such a specimen go, now could I?"

They all smiled at one another. "So I followed him and lured him into my car where Lugar"—he nodded to the sadistic keeper—"was conveniently hidden in the back seat. The rest is obvious."

"You say that this one was Mr. Benson's slave?" Hans nodded in answer to the other model's question. "That's strange," he said thoughtfully. "I always heard he was a top himself. Now you say he was a slave."

"These Americans," Hans said disgustedly. "They're always into their macho trip, thinking that they have to cover the true desires of their wretched souls."

Hans walked away; the rest followed quickly, but the model lingered, ever so slightly, staring into the cell at the three of us. His departure was a signal to let us all breathe a little more easily.

"What if they test you?" Rocco asked.

"Yeah, what if they try to see if you can get it up?"

"That's why Mr. Benson put me through those motions," the blond said. His tone was unconvincing.

"What do you mean?"

"Well." The model tried to regain his composure. "Mr. Benson thought that if I could fool Jamie and make him believe I got off on being a bottom...well, I could fool anyone." He tried to make his explanation complete.

"And you did fool even me," I added.

"Right." The blond's answer was too quick and satisfied. He started to walk away, as though his motion would change the subject. I looked at Rocco; a smile started to unfold on his face, making me break into loud, uncontrollable guffaws that hurt my bruised back with their quick, jerky motion. It suddenly became clear to us. The epitome of American manhood swiveled around and looked at us with this blank expression on his face that was soon covered by a growing tide of red color that spread across his face and down his naked chest. "Okay, fellas, okay." He knew that we knew! The flush deepened and then, slowly, a smile appeared on his own expression and he started a slight, ever so slight, giggle.

"No one, but no one, could fool Jamie about being a bottom." Rocco spit the words out between the louder laughs.

"I know." The voice seemed so small for such a big man. "I know, Jesus, though I never knew it could be like that. Kneeling and having someone standing over you." His voice was more solemn. "It was a revelation." He regained himself still once more. "Well, guys, let's just say that we won't have to worry about any tests. Every time I think of Mr. Benson and all the men in the club, little ole Nellie here"—he lifted his flaccid tool—"stands to attention." We looked down to see the fabled cock slowly rise up, filling with the memories of Mr. Benson we both shared.

That might have been the only white man's cock that Rocco couldn't resist. Few could. It was molded to perfection. Its veins stood out from the shaft as the prick grew in dimension, the deep red head engorged into a perfect plum shape. Rocco's eyes started to glaze over at the sight. I remembered Mr. Benson's even more perfect penis and was content just to feel a closeness to this man who understood Mr. Benson's power. He and I embraced tightly. I'm sure he knew why. As our arms went softly around each other, I felt the hair on the top of Rocco's head push between my legs and heard him slurping up that rigid pole.

The three of us fell back on the foam pad that passed for a bed. I was just glad to have welcome arms around me, comforting me after all I had been through. Rocco was more demanding as he slid up and down the long prick.

Our kisses were deep and warm after what I had been through. Their welcome comfort enveloped me, as his arms gently caressed my sore back. "Give me your cock, Jamie," he moaned, Rocco's mouth doing as much to affect him as my emotions. I smiled in acknowledgment and rose up to deliver my shorn dick into his hairy opening. I lay on my side, letting him have his way with my suddenly hard cock, watching his pelvis, with those fabulous thigh muscles pushing it, pump into Rocco's waiting and eager face. Their bodies both contracted, their stomachs tensed, and Rocco's face bobbed more quickly in time with his own fist flying on his own cock. Then...they spasmed together, each of their loads shooting off with necessary release.

I assured them that I was fine. My half-hard cock didn't need any more than their friendship now. It felt so good to curl up between the two of them with our three sets of arms around one another. We were each so different, different looking, different acting, but we were each bound together in some special kind of knowledge. We were together in our lives.

We stayed there, cuddled, for a while, listening to the other voices in the long, narrow cell room. Finally I said, "When can you activate your message?"

The model—I had finally learned his name was Rick—said, "We have to wait until we know what the whole thing's about. You see, these guys haven't just recently been disappearing. They go in waves. There's some reason, some destination, and I have to find out what and where."

"You mean, we may have to stay here and put up with that smelly cock for a week?" Rocco was horrified.

"I'm afraid so. As much as I like you guys"—he squeezed our shoulders into his own—"and as much as Mr. Benson and Brendan are going to be worried, I just can't let the whole thing go down the tubes. We have to know more about the operation."

Rocco and I moaned. The noisy door opened again at the end of the hall and the dark-haired model came up the passageway, Hans trailing behind him.

"Abdul, of course you can test him. But he's such a fine specimen, you mustn't hurt him."

"I don't think I'll have to," the scented voice replied, his eyes having caught Rocco and me huddled up in Rick's arms. "Your man has already found a way."

"What?" asked Hans.

They were standing in front of us now. "There are two things, Klaus. First, he is supposed to be a bottom now, or so you say. And second, he has obviously made friends with his other Topmen slave friends. Very well." He turned sharply to Rick. "On your feet, slave. We are going to give you the thrill of your life. You are going to get to satisfy my prick."

The dark-haired man folded his arms over his chest and waited as Rick slowly got to his feet and went to the bars.

"Fuck you," he spat.

"Listen to me, you pale imitation of masculinity," the dark man sputtered back. "Your tattooed friend is going to receive whatever punishment you or your scarred friend deserve while you're here. You had better remember that before you speak to your master that way."

Rick looked at Rocco, who had doubled over into the corner. He needed no explanation of Rocco's weaknesses. He looked at me; we shared the knowledge that it was time for a real bottom to take action. The blond man sank to his feet. "Yes, Master," he barely whispered.

The mustached face smiled in victory. "Bring the three of them upstairs to my quarters, in chains. I'll take care to make sure that this is really a bottom and not some trick being played on us."

"You want all three?" asked Hans.

"Of course, you frigid Germans wouldn't understand that a real man needs more than a single bottom to play with, and in this case, I need one to control with." Hans went stiff with anger. "Don't try try to start anything, Herr Klaus, this is my show, too. I want the three of them brought to me now."

In another half hour, we were led out of the cell

block; the jealous eyes of the other inmates followed us as we walked the hall and went through the door. When we left the original room we found ourselves in another nondescript area, again walled by concrete. Each of our necks was joined to the other by a heavy metal chain linking collars around our necks. Our hands were manacled behind our backs and another link of the chain went down to our ankles. The lengths of metal were so short that our steps were limited to a shuffle.

We went down a step of stairs, then up another, and soon found ourselves walking into a room that was furnished luxuriously, so much a contrast to the barren spaces we had walked through. There was a non-Western air to the space; there were no pieces of regular furniture, but rather large, opulent pillows strewn across the floor. The walls were hung with rich oriental carpets. There were round brass tables placed here and there. The scene was like something out of *A Thousand and One Nights*, and it dawned on me: Abdul was Arab! I looked at Rick's puzzled face and saw a kind of recognition come over him, too.

And at the same time we each stiffened. This was the real thing. *This was slavery*.

Abdul sat in the midst of a large mound of pillows and sucked on a water pipe. Three young, pretty, and, of course, blond young men moved about him silently and kept their eyes averted from ours.

He had changed into a native costume, the many folds of cloth seeming strange after he had just appeared in Levi's only moments ago. "You see me in my natural habitat." He smiled. His hands clapped almost soundlessly and there were sudden motions as two enormous Nubians, their ebony skin oiled to a bright glistening shine, stepped out from the shadows. Rocco's knees quivered.

"Get out." He bit off words to the jailers who had brought us there. "That one"—Abdul pointed to Rocco—"put him on the horse."

There was no reason or way even to try to resist as the two giants took Rocco out of the metal restraints and led him to the corner where there was a large leather-covered device. They took his yielding limbs—poor Rocco, he could never have resisted those two—and stretched him against the corners, where they fastened his wrists and ankles again.

"Let me be very clear." Abdul started talking again. "Your friend is in no great pain, I assure you. His position involves no stress, and his seating is better and more comfortable than your cell. However, all I need do is raise my hand"—he flicked his wrist up to show us—"and he will be beaten." A loud, bestial cry came from Rocco's corner as one of the Nubians stood holding a menacing, many-pronged whip that had obviously just visited Rocco's backside.

"You, you will obey my every order, or *he* will be beaten." The wrist flicked again and Rocco's screams filled the room again to underline the point. I knew Rocco couldn't take much of this. I had to act. I strode across to where Abdul sat, dragging Rick in the clanking chains, and knelt before him, the joining chain forcing a not-very-willing Rick down on his own knees.

"We understand, Sir." My head was bowed as I spoke. I heard a muffled assent from Rick right after I had finished. He also must have realized Rocco's plight. I was thankful for Mr. Benson's having trained him enough to know that he should take a position of subservience right now and not try anything foolish.

"I am very pleased." The foreign accent clipped off the words. "I want nothing more than decent, hard-working slaves for my pleasure...and for the marketplace. There is no reason to destroy that one in the corner, even if he is unfortunately marked. But you two"—a long-tongued fly swatter came out and brushed my head—"you two are such fine examples of Americana, that you must be held in reserve for the finest of customers.

"You may look up at me." I couldn't really see Rick's motions, but took the absence of punishment as a sign he was going through with it.

"Most of my friends, as I, appreciate the gentle beauty of fair-haired younger boys." Smiling, he grabbed one of the young men who had been in the room before we arrived. The kid only had a loincloth to cover his nakedness. He was the kind of blond whose hair is unnaturally light, and whose skin bronzes when exposed to the sun. His blue eyes shone out from the light brown skin. "But all of us appreciate, as well, the symbol of training as well learned as yours is supposed to be." The fly swatter again brushed against my head. "And none would deny the satisfaction a man feels when he knows that he holds one of the very symbols of American manhood in his power." The swatter disappeared from my view; I'm sure it must have been showing Rick his special place in the universe.

Abdul turned from us and called the three young men over to him. "These new slaves have been kept in the dungeon with the animals. You must make them presentable for household work. I want each of them cleaned up and the one with the scars taken care of. The one in the corner...ignore.

"Follow these three, they will take care of you," Abdul said, and then suddenly warned, "Do not try anything foolish, or your friend will pay." And again the wrist flicked and Rocco's scream filled the air.

Rick and I were unshackled and led behind a

183

screen to another room, a bathroom, with a huge circular tub in the center. The three men refused to talk to us, or even to look us in the eye. "Rick, what does this mean? Why did he pull us out of the dungeon?"

"Just like Mr. Benson thought they would, they're testing me, seeing if I really am a bottom, Jamie."

"There's no test, Rick. I mean, don't they know that you're doing all this for Rocco?"

"No, Jamie, they're not just seeing if you and I will follow orders. They're checking out our attitude. I'm very glad you're along, kid."

"You are?"

The three led us mutely to the pool and into the warm, luxurious water. We didn't speak until they were again away from hearing range.

"Sure I'm glad, Jamie. I never would have been able to get even this far. I would have stayed there and just waited for orders. That's not what they want; they want a slave's attitude, like when you went and knelt, and made me follow. That was perfect, Jamie, and it probably saved our lives."

I was very thankful for all Mr. Benson's training at that moment. I sank into the bubbling water and tried to think, how can we ever get out of this?

TEN

A growing sense of anxiety came over me as the boys cleaned us off after our bath. We had assumed that Rick was to be tested, but I wondered. The testing had been done. There was something else going on. I looked over at his ruggedly handsome face and wonderfully strong body. The face, beautiful though it may have been, was much older than these other boys', or my own for that matter. Rick was definitely a man's man in appearance. His size and stature made him tower over the rest of us. What did Abdul have in mind?

The blond boys remained silent. When we were dried, I expected them to give us a loincloth like their own. But no, they motioned for us to follow them back into the main room where Abdul waited, an evil smile again on his face. We were so concerned with him that it took us a moment to see the contraption that had arrived during our absence.

There, stretched before Abdul, was the dildo equipment that the blond cellmate had warned us about. There were a dozen protruding prongs, each larger than the preceding. They started with a size that seemed almost within the range of reason, but then quickly increased in size till the last one, which had to be beyond human endurance. I stared at the torture devices.

"You are intrigued?" Abdul asked.

"No, Sir."

"You will be—soon." He motioned for the Nubians to come forward out of the shadows. "The little one goes first."

They grabbed me. I flashed on struggling, but there was no use. One forced me to bend over while the other took a handful of grease and wiped it up and down my ass. He took more and coated the first three dildos.

"Start," ordered Abdul.

I went over to the first one and bent. It was knee height, I squatted onto it and felt the wooden handle going up against my sphincter. I breathed deeply and got it up past the first ring of tight muscles. The height between the top and the base was only about a foot. It slid in fairly easily.

Oh, thank God for Mr. Benson's training!

I pulled up and waited. Abdul simply pointed to the next dildo. Again I squatted down and let the phallus rest against my asshole, concentrating to try to relax the tight muscles. Again it slid through, but this time with a sharp burst of pain when I had gotten down to the base. "Stay there until Mr. Rhinestone Cowboy tests himself on the first." He turned away from me and toward Rick. "Your friend, no matter how well he is trained, will begin to feel great pain. He will not be allowed to stand until you have impaled yourself on the first prong. Do it!"

Rick looked at the dildo. He went over and went through the humiliating motions of having the Nubians grease him up. The stretching inside me did begin to hurt. He went over to the nearby spike and tried to copy my moves. His mouth opened in obvious pain as the polished wood disappeared inside him. Sweat rolled down to his sides; his breathing was deep. But he did it. We both looked to Abdul. "The next one."

I had to go through the first four dildos that first time. Somehow Rick made it to the third. His groans had become audible as the wide part pushed apart his ass. I myself was sweating profusely now. The pressure made it feel as though my gut would burst, but there was some kind of victory in our accomplishment. I wondered if Rick was thinking of Mr. Benson. Did it help him to remember the master as it helped me?

We both stood, our chests bellowing for air. "You are both surprisingly good," said Abdul. "You"—he pointed to me—"are going to make an excellent slave. I can now see you squatting on the cocks of tribesmen with great ease, giving them great pleasure."

He turned to Rick; the smile increased in its ominous character. "It is unfortunate that you will not be able to give them the same pleasure."

Rick was puzzled. "What do you mean? I did it, didn't I, Sir? I passed the test."

"But the test wasn't really for you. Your part in it was simply for my pleasure. You have no idea what great satisfaction it gave me to see the well-known symbol of American manhood fitting an Arab dildo up his fine ass. No, my friend, it is not the will of Allah for you to be a sex slave. There are more important tasks for a man of your size to perform."

"Sir?" Rick asked.

"Every sheik must have a well-guarded harem. It must be staffed by the most powerful and skilled and forceful"—he paused as he cleaned a fingernail with his fruit knife—"eunuchs." The face rose up to smile directly at Rick.

We were stunned by the news. Rick went pale with fear. How could he get to Mr. Benson? He said he had a way. Was there time?

The Nubians came up quickly and grabbed Rick's arms. Handcuffs were attached and ankle chains clasped before either of us knew what to do. They held the bound model in their grip as Abdul came down off his pillowed podium. He walked up to Rick and cheerfully grabbed hold of those beautiful fuzz-covered orbs of his. He let them rest in his palm; he carefully and slowly lifted them, then rotated them in his hand.

"What would America think of this, huh?" The smile on Abdul's face was sickening in its pleasure. He took out the fruit knife that he had had in his hand. It had a curved Syrian blade. He put it down to Rick's balls and scraped the surface. The blade was so sharp it took off some of the incredibly fine yellow hair. He transferred the golden testicles from his palm to the dull outside of the blade. "If I were simply to turn this blade over, my dear friend, you would lose your most prized possession. How do you feel?"

Sweat was pouring down Rick's face and into his mustache. The liquid oozed from his pores and ran down the side of his muscled stomach in streams. "Please, Sir," he whispered, "I'll do anything, Sir. Please." He could barely be heard.

"But you would do anything, anyhow. Don't you know that you have abandoned all hope?"

Suddenly he stepped away. I gasped. Did he? I looked at Rick's balls, pulled up by the tension and the fright, but still attached to his body. "do not worry yet. I would not risk such a valuable investment with a kitchen knife. There will be a doctor who will be happy to have the honor of removing the testicles of this asshole. He will probably eat them for dinner in front of you. He is"—that smile again—"very kinky. But later."

The situation was becoming hopeless. Rick without balls? John Wayne without balls was as likely. Had he signaled Mr. Benson yet? We were taken off to the corner where Rocco was stretched out. They threw Rick down on the floor. I collapsed on top of him, holding my arms around his huge chest, rubbing my face into that gorgeous body hair. "Oh, Rick, it'll be okay. I'm sure Mr. Benson will get here in time."

"I certainly hope so. Jesus, my balls!"

"Rick," I whispered, "have you called him yet?"

"Yes," Rick answered, "I just hope he finds us with half the U.S. Cavalry alongside him."

I looked over to Rocco's worried eyes. There was nothing any of us could do but wait.

An hour later, Abdul reappeared. "The two of them, bring them in for a viewing. We have customers, gentlemen."

Another mystery. What was this to be about? The Nubians chained me and loosened the ankle restraints on Rick. We followed them out and down the corridor. There was still no indication of where we were. We were led into still another room. It was more of a hall, with high ceilings and rugs hanging down from the walls. The three blond slave boys stood behind Abdul. His back was to the far wall. At an angle to him sat about two dozen Arabs, all in traditional dress, all sitting on the same large kind of pillows. Along the far wall, now directly in front of us, were the blonds from downstairs. All of them were naked and chained. I suddenly realized that this was the slave auction.

At a nod from Abdul, the first young man was led

up onto the podium, a stagelike affair, by Hans. His hands were attached by cuffs behind his back. "And this, gentlemen, is one of the very fine specimens we have. All will give you great pleasure in your palaces and tents." The men on the pillows nodded; a few made remarks to one another as the first boy was turned around, his fine melon ass displayed. He was forced to bend over and spread his legs to reveal his asshole. Hans stuck the handle of the marker he held in his hand right up the guy's butt.

"All of this shipment has been trained for your convenience. Their love holes have been stretched to spare you any discomfort." An appreciative noise came up from the audience. I couldn't see any of their faces underneath the volumes of their headgear.

Each of the men in front of us was put through the same humiliation. Only one dared to resist at all. His strange-sounding Brooklyn-accented voice demanded his constitutional rights. He claimed to be the free-born son of a Norwegian immigrant to this country. No one could take him away. The crowd laughed uproariously. They found it amusing. Hans found it very unamusing and beat the boy repeatedly with his stick until he squelched the flow of words and produced a silence of sobs and a rush of marks on the young man's back. "An unfortunate malcontent, gentlemen. He will be kept here and given special training."

"Gentlemen," piped up Abdul. "You may want to put in a special bid for this one. 'Special training' means that he will experience a number of weeks in my household. After which even the most tiresome slave becomes docile and loving. Let me show you." Abdul snapped his fingers and one of the three boys beside him went down on his knees and parted the long robe to reveal Abdul's heralded cock. He quickly sucked on it, soon producing the famous hard-on. Another snap of the fingers and a second boy came round, whipped off his loincloth and with unbelievable speed sat straight down on the huge member, pumping away at the dick that had cost so many their freedom.

"These two once tried to escape. They even dared to raise a hand to their master. Now…" A hand went out and grabbed hard at the first boy's ballsac, twisting it with such obvious force that great pain must have resulted, but only a slight grimace appeared on his face. "Now they do my bidding with the greatest of ease."

Another appreciative murmur went through the audience. If those had been delinquent slaves, then obviously Abdul knew his business. I doubted at that moment if even I could have performed that way for Mr. Benson.

The crowd was enraptured by the scene of Abdul's fine cock as it kept disappearing into the blond ass, and the face of the other boy as Abdul continued his slow, hard torture. "Go on," he ordered Hans, obviously aware that his performance was turning on the audience and making it probable that an even better sale would be made.

"Gentlemen, the boys you have just seen will be sold at auction today. Their arrival in the Middle East is guaranteed. Now we have two special specimens for your approval."

Suddenly the Nubians gathered up my arms and were dragging me to the stage. I was there staring down at the crowd, shivering with the large room's draft and my own fear. "This is one of the very special products of this country, sirs, something that few places besides my own beloved Germany can offer. The masochist slave. This one, gentlemen, is for your *very* special enjoyment. For those of you who can appreciate the sight of a bright red welt growing on a young, rounded ass. I can attest myself to his willingness and enjoyment at being mishandled and hurt." His hand came out and twisted cruelly at my tit. It played with that oh-so-sensitive part of my body so carefully trained by Mr. Benson. In spite of the cold and the fear and the eyes of the onlookers, my cock started to rise at the sensation. I blushed as the audience reacted to me as though I were some kind of freak.

"Unfortunately," Hans continued when he had made his point, "some unknown person has misused this fine piece of property." He swiveled me around to show the marks on my back, still there from the other night's beating. "But I assure you they will disappear. Until, that is, you choose to repeat them." Another sound from the audience.

"And last, gentlemen, we offer another specialty. One of America's most famous faces."

Rick was half-carried, half-led up the stairs to join me. His face was full of the embarrassment that Hans was purposefully laying on him. "This specimen"—the loudest noise yet went up as the men apparently recognized Rick's well-photographed face—"will be delivered to you as a eunuch." The first truly loud sound came from the audience.

Hans tugged hard on Rick's balls and stretched them painfully to their forward limit. "These, the sorry excuse for America's masculine symbol, will be expertly and carefully severed from the body. You may give your harem a gift of infinite beauty and infinite safety."

Spontaneous applause went up from the pillows as though it were a fashion show where the top of the line was being modeled, not a man's manhood!

Abdul stopped his display and wrapped his garment back around himself. "And so, the auction. Each of the men has been given a number. You must each bid in order."

I felt tremendous defeat as the bidding began. It seemed too unreal to be in New York City and to be sold to Arab potentates at auction. And Rick's balls! And where was Mr. Benson? Could he ever save us from this?

"Okay, that's enough. You're under arrest. Hands in the air."

A shocked sound went through the assembly as four of the Arab men suddenly stood and pulled guns from under their robes. I knew the voice. Brendan!

The buyers had all stood in a panic and thrown their hands in the air. Strange languages shouted out in cries that sounded like begging for mercy. Abdul bolted upright and leapt onto the stage with his fruit knife in his hand. The closest of the four men had seen him start and raced up to jump in front of him before he could reach us. The two men crouched and began to circle one another. "Jamie, get Rick off the stage."

Mr. Benson!

I pushed, shoved, and carried Rick down the steps as we watched the spectacle before us. "The rest of you stay still!" Brendan commanded. Everyone's hands were still in the air. The other two men came over and disarmed the Nubians while Hans stood stock still at the rear of the stage.

As the two combatants circled, Mr. Benson carefully threw off the outer layers of the confining Arab costume. Abdul thought he had Mr. Benson off-guard and swiped at him with the super-sharp knife. Mr. Benson jumped back just in time and used the wasted motion to toss off the last of the clothes above his waist. His magnificent body shone in the light as the sweat glistened on his body hair.

"Put down the knife, you idiot," he ordered.

Abdul answered with another sortie at Mr. Benson's midsection. I gasped as it came too close for my comfort to opening up his beloved stomach. But this time, freed of the clothing, Mr. Benson never let Abdul recover. He followed through with a sharp karate cut on the back of the Arab's neck and sent him sprawling onto the floor. He stood, breathing deeply, and turned to face the audience. He nodded to Brendan, who began spouting off the Miranda code.

I raced to meet Mr. Benson halfway as he strode over to me. I grabbed him by the waist and buried my face in his chest. Tears of relief spread down my cheeks. "Oh, Mr. Benson, I'm so glad to see you."

"What the hell are you doing here?" He didn't respond to me, but rested his fists on his waist. Through my tears I told him the story—it must have sounded incoherent that time—about the sadist who had beaten me, about the gangster who had warmed me, about Rick and Hans and Abdul. "You silly ass. I'll deal with you later," was his only response.

He went over and found the quaking Hans still against the wall at the rear of the stage. "You traitor," Mr. Benson spat. "How could you have done this to the Topmen? Do you know what kind of bad publicity this is going to mean? And the worst part is Jersey City! Did you have to do it in Jersey City? Do you know what the media is going to do with a story about a slave ring selling blond boys to Arabs in *Jersey City*?" He screamed at Hans so loudly his face went red and the veins stood out on his neck. Then he was quieter and started to nod his head back and forth. "Jesus Christ. No class at all."

The three men down on the floor were rounding up the suspects and handcuffing them all. Brendan had produced a walkie-talkie and was barking orders into it, obviously demanding reinforcements.

In a matter of a few minutes, the place was swarming with blue-coated police, pushing and shoving the Arabs. Brendan came up on the stage, relieved of his duties. "You won't believe this, Mr. Benson, but probably all of those guys are going to go free."

"What for?" Mr. Benson asked indignantly.

"They're almost all covered by diplomatic immunity. If they're not at the U.N. or Washington, they're members of a royal family. Shit, at least we got these characters, and the good name of the Topmen back."

"But the publicity. Can't you see the headlines now, MILLIONAIRES' CLUB CAUGHT SELLING SLAVES IN JERSEY CITY?"

"No sweat, Mr. Benson. They'll never read a word of this in the newspapers."

"How are you going to arrange that?" Mr. Benson challenged.

"I won't have to," answered Brendan. "Those boys we just arrested already own half the newspapers in the country; they'll just buy whatever else they need to keep it quiet. It's very important to their national image that slavery not be mentioned. They and their friends will see that their image is left intact."

"Well, that's a relief," said Mr. Benson. "It would have killed me. I don't know if the slavery's so bad," he repeated in a disbelieving low voice. "But *Jersey City*?"

A couple hours later, Abdul and Hans were safely locked away in a Jersey City cell and Rick, Mr. Benson, and I were in the penthouse on Fifth Avenue.

I never dreamed I would be so happy to see the place. I stripped as soon as we got in and dropped down on one of Mr. Benson's familiar boots, desperately pleased to be home.

I was licking away at the leather when his voice boomed out, "I'm waiting for a reason as to why you were there."

"Mr. Benson, Sir, Rocco had said, well he had said you had taken Rick for your slave and kicked me out and that's why I thought you had given me the money, and so I was really unhappy and I met this man and he beat me badly, and then Rocco and I got drunk and we ran into Hans."

"Why didn't you stay in a hotel?"

"You never actually told me to stay away from Rocco, Sir."

"What a mess," he sighed.

"And you, why didn't you tell me as soon as Jamie was there?" He had turned on a very nervous Rick.

"Mr. Benson, I thought you'd want me to go through with it. I didn't think he'd be in any trouble."

"Well, he's safe, but it was an asshole thing to do. The one who's probably in real trouble is Rocco. I bet Brendan beats him bloody." He changed the subject suddenly. "Jamie, get me a drink."

I scurried up and went to the liquor closet and poured his Black Label scotch. "You and Rick too, I suppose you could both use one about now."

I was thankful for the offer. Rick came over and helped himself. He followed me back over to where Mr. Benson sat in his favorite chair. I handed Mr. Benson his drink and sank thankfully onto the floor by my master's feet.

Home at last!

I sipped on the liquor and looked up at Mr. Benson. He was deep in thought. "I'm relieved, Rick, that you caught the guys. Any trouble with the alarm?"

"No." Rick blushed scarlet. "Actually, Abdul set it off."

"How?"

Rick told the story of the pegs we had been forced to squat on. Mr. Benson laughed as I did when I realized that the alarm had been implanted deep inside Rick's asshole and that the wooden peg had touched it on the last and biggest dildo.

Rick and I started to tell Mr. Benson all about the ring. "Did you ever suspect Abdul?"

"No, I never did," Rick answered Mr. Benson's question. "He's always had a lot of money and I knew he was gay. But he makes so much modeling, it never dawned on me that he would need to do something like this."

"Must have been very greedy," replied Mr. Benson.

"Rick, why aren't you sitting down?" Mr. Benson's tone of voice had changed from the conversational level he had been using. There was an edge to his voice now, almost challenging.

Rick blushed again. He sputtered a bit and finally said, "I'm not sure where I should sit."

"The floor." Mr. Benson looked directly at him.

"Yes, Sir," Rick answered, and he sank to the ground, his eyes not returning either of our looks.

"Now, doesn't that feel better?" Mr. Benson was using his training voice.

From his kneeling position, Rick answered, "Yes, Sir."

Mr. Benson was looking very thoughtful and I was feeling very nervous. The make-believe slave Rick had threatened me enough; I didn't need to deal with the real slave Rick, not in my own home. How could I say anything to Mr. Benson while he was still angry about my going out and being captured? He suddenly smiled and reached out a hand to pat my head. It felt so good to see his face like that and to feel his hand on my body in that quiet, gentle way that I just sort of collapsed against him and rubbed my head against his knee.

"The whole reason I got into this adventure was to save slaves from evil masters. I guess the least I can do now is find a good slave a good master." He stood up and went to the phone. I could tell that Rick was straining as hard as I was to hear what he said, but his voice was so low we didn't catch a single word.

When he had hung up the phone, he returned to us. He assumed his top role with a firm "Get out of those clothes, asshole," at Rick. I watched as once again that beautiful blond body was stripped of its covering and the fuzzy ass once again went up in the air while his head went to Mr. Benson's feet.

"Jamie, we're going to have company. Lots of it. I want you at your best. You must need a shave. Do it! You"—he looked down at Rick—"shower in Jamie's room and get yourself ready. You think you've discovered a new part of yourself. You've just begun. There's a much more real adventure coming your way this night."

Rick and I ran madly around trying to prepare for this surprise evening. I was interested in the excited way he greeted the sudden commands. I mentioned it to him. He replied, "Jamie, ever since that first night here, when you and Mr. Benson showed me the ropes, I've been thinking about it." He paused as he dried himself off with a towel. The beautiful nakedness turned me on; I was remembering fucking that ass! "And I'm tired of thinking about it. You know, I'm this famous model, right? And all these people want me. Most of them want me to fuck them, given my image and everything, but nothing has ever seemed as natural to me as the night Mr. Benson had me down on the floor, fucking the ass of mine he had just beaten. I might as well admit who and what I am, Jamie."

I understood perfectly.

Within an hour, Rick and I were naked and standing in front of Mr. Benson, our clean bodies pink with scrubbing and our faces bright with anticipation. Mr. Benson was obviously fixing Rick up—he was excited by the prospect of a man, and I was delighted with the prospect of getting rid of him. I liked him well enough, mind you, but it was definitely time for him to go on.

Mr. Benson motioned me over to him and put an arm around my waist, cupping one of my clean-shaven ass cheeks. "Feel good, boy?"

"Yes, Sir!" I nearly yelled as an answer and then I threw my arms around his neck and pressed my body against his warmth. "Oh, Mr. Benson, I'm so glad to be back with you."

"Enough, enough." His gruff voice protested the intimacy very unconvincingly. I had been thinking about the danger he had put himself through for me, and the lengths he had gone to protect me with the whole masquerade of Rick's initiation. "There is a point in all this, Jamie, where I am very, very disappointed in you."

"Sir?" I was crestfallen.

"Jamie, you didn't trust me. You questioned my actions and motivations. That is very unbecoming behavior."

I hung my head in shame. All he had done for me, but he was right when he pointed out what I had not done for him. "I'm sorry, Sir."

"Before the others get here, Jamie, I want to know if you are going to give up this foolish and destructive questioning from now on. Will you trust me for the rest of our time together?"

"Oh, yes, Sir!" I meant it, too!

He looked at me long and hard. "You had better, Jamie. I've put a lot of work into you. I want no more foolishness, understand?"

"Yes, Sir!"

He turned. "And you, Rick. Are you finished with these silly games you've been playing about being top, bottom, around or whatever? Are you serious about knowing what you want now?"

Rick was embarrassed and looked down. "Yes, Mr. Benson. I know who I am. I'm willing to live up to it and try to make good at it."

"If you have any sense at all, you're going to go through what I've set up for you tonight. No questions now. Just trust me and follow your orders. One thing you've got to learn is that sometimes you just have to let the top take control."

"Yes, Sir."

The doorbell rang. "Get it, Jamie."

I ran over to the door and opened it to find the always-handsome Brendan standing there in that wonderful Topmen uniform. Behind him stood the not-so-happy–looking Rocco. They stepped in and Rick and Rocco and I went through the greetings, kissing the feet of the tops. Brendan was obviously in a foul mood.

"Do you believe the danger these idiots put themselves in? Absolute idiocy. Drinking." He spat, looking at a terrified Rocco. "This one is going to end up with his ass in a sling for a good month. Luckily *Roots* is being rerun next week." Rocco shook with fear. "At least by the time I'm finished with him, he'll be done with this fantasy of not 'really' being a bottom, just play-acting for me. If he can stick it out, he's going to be beaten into ten different kinds of submission." Brendan's nostrils flared.

"Now, Brendan," Mr. Benson began. "The boys were only being stupid. They meant well."

"Damn stupid," shot back Brendan. "It just pisses me off to have to deal with this one's idiocy, Mr. Benson." He looked at Rocco again. "Idiot!" he screamed.

Rocco, Rick, and I all jumped at the yell. Poor Rocco looked as though he had already received a less-than-friendly welcome home. His ass was covered with even more welts than the Nubians had given him. A tear started from his eye; he went over to Brendan and got on his knees and wrapped himself around Brendan's legs. "Please, please forgive me, Sir. I'm sorry. It won't happen again."

Brendan smiled a play-acting stereotypical smile at Mr. Benson. "Nothin' does my heart as much good as a honky at his black master's feet." He had to give up the hard tone and reached down and patted Rocco's head. "It really is difficult to keep a slave sometimes, Mr. Benson."

"Well, Brendan, with Rick here, it looks like we won't be the only ones to know about it."

Brendan smiled at the beautiful model who had been trying to keep in the background. "It sure is funny how long it takes some of these bottoms to come out of their closets, isn't it?" The two tops laughed a private joke to one another.

The doorbell rang again. I started to go to answer it. Mr. Benson stopped me. "I'll get that. You get over with Rick and sit in the corner. I want no noise from you two.

"You too," Brendan said to Rocco.

201

The three of us went over to the corner Mr.
Benson had pointed out and sat expectantly. What
was Rick's fate to be? Mr. Benson opened the door
and in walked Frank and Sal, the hunky lovers who
were both Topmen. They were still dressed for the
construction job they worked together: dusty clothes
and roughly worn boots and construction helmets.
Hard-working sweat had left rivulets of dirt tracked
down their pumped-up arms and had matted the
thick chest hair that came out over the top of their
sweatshirts.

"What's the rush, Mr. Benson? Brendan called
us." Frank recognized the man whose name he had
just mentioned. "Oh, hi, Brendan." He and Sal
flashed matching white-toothed smiles at the police-
man. "Well, Brendan said you wanted us to come
over right away. We didn't even have time to
change." He was voicing the obvious.

Rocco and I exchanged knowing glances at one
another. Them! Was Rick ready for this? I remembered the night that Mr. Benson had taken me to the
clubhouse and had let all the Topmen use my body.
They had been there and had stood over me, kissing
one another while I was forced to suck first one's cock
and then the other's. My own prick now rose in memory of the feeling of kneeling before the two men who
would have to be considered the best-looking of the
Topmen, though I would never say that to Mr. Benson.

"Come and have a drink and I'll explain." They, of
course, wanted beer. I ran to the kitchen and brought
back two cold cans. I found them eyeing Rick specu-
latively. They stared at him and then at one another.
Their common looks had a twinkling in the eyes; they
obviously appreciated him. Probably all the more
since he was aware of their looks and was attractively
blushing at the attention they were paying.

"Okay, you two. All of us at the club have been worried. We don't know how you two get on together. You're both so adamantly tops that you can hardly be getting sex from one another..."

"That's not true, Mr. Benson. I mean, we make out together," Sal said quietly.

"What, beating off?" Mr. Benson was openly unimpressed.

"As bad for two tops to beat one another off as for two bottoms to bump pussies," interjected Brendan. "You two got to resolve your relationship."

"We've tried almost everything," said Frank, admitting a problem.

"Yes, once I even let this one fuck me," Sal added. Mr. Benson's eyebrows went up at the thought of one of his Topmen being fucked, but he decided to hold his peace.

"Look, I have the answer for you. One of your problems is that you're both too pretty. You can have anyone you want, but you hardly ever find anyone as attractive as the other one is." The couple nodded in agreement. I thought it must be a great dilemma for them. "Now here," Mr. Benson finally acknowledged Rick to the company, "is someone as attractive as you guys. He wants to be a slave to someone. But if we send him out on the streets or fix him up with one of the other guys at the club, he'll feel the same way you two do—no one will satisfy him. Okay, the answer is obvious. He becomes your joint slave. Only the two of you put together will be so attractive that he'll be able to have the proper attitude of a slave: only the pair of you will make him feel lucky enough to be your slave that he'll keep working to make you happy."

"Isn't that true, Rick? Wouldn't it make you happy to be able to service these two hunks every day?"

Brendan asked the model. Rick barely heard him speak, he was staring so hard and had that special glazed look on his face. The two men who sat on the couch really *were* the image of manhood in America, not just the plastic representation that he and Abdul had stood in as. Their hairy, muscled bodies, the heavy filled crotch of their workpants, the thick curly hair, all of it combined with the smell of men at work to leave Rick with a growing crotch and the beginning of a need to please that Rocco and I now acknowledged to one another with a meaningful stare.

"Yes, Sir, I would be glad to serve those men, Sir." Rick could hardly whisper the words. I smiled, knowing that in his mind were images of himself impaled on Frank's cock while he sucked mightily on Sal's uncut dong.

All in all, I thought it was the happiest ending that could have come out of Mr. Benson and me. I was delighted with Rick's new life, and especially since it didn't include living with Mr. Benson. I was safe in the penthouse, kneeling at the feet of the master who had meant so much to me and who had rescued me from a life in the Middle East as an Arab's slave. I cuddled up against Mr. Benson, thinking the night was over and that I could now get ready to sleep.

"Then that's settled," said Mr. Benson. "Now we have one more agenda. Jamie, over against the wall, stretch out your arms." His voice took a quick military turn. "Move," he yelled. I jumped up and went over the the wall, the scene of the horrendous torture sessions when Mr. Benson had trained my tits. I spread my arms. He had followed me and brought the restraints with him. In a few seconds, my arms and legs were stretched to their limits. The whole group had their eyes on me. I wasn't prepared for this. Was he going to pull a public scene on me? It seemed so inappropriate to the gathering.

"It seems that Jamie, even after weeks, months of training, still has some insecurities about his status around here. Enough so that a single rumor by a silly slave"—Brendan and Mr. Benson both glared at Rocco—"can send him into a panic. I'll have none of that.

"Part of my initial response was to beat him." He turned back to me and looked into my face. "But I realized that that wouldn't do the trick. What I needed was some way to show him that he's mine and that I mean to keep him. Something like another brand, which should have done the job but which obviously didn't.

"Jamie," he addressed me now. "There's no ritual for a master and a slave that we alone know about. I mean, no way to tie the bond that a straight couple might have in a marriage. But I've decided to create one just for you."

I would have felt much more comfortable and much happier about this little speech if I hadn't been in the particular position I was in. I didn't expect a love soliloquy while spread-eagled against a brick wall. The glint of metal in Mr. Benson's hand didn't make me any more comfortable. At least, though, I didn't know what he was doing when he grabbed my tit and there was this sudden sense of pressure and then a shrill, hard-edged wave of intense pain. I called out in agony at the sight of blood coming from my chest when Mr. Benson finally pulled away.

My tears couldn't stop the irrational questioning of what he was doing. Through my tears I saw the smiles of the other men; they all looked so pleased. After Rocco and Rick and I had gone through so much, now they abandoned me to this torture? I was hurt until I looked down at the bleeding tit.

There, through the slowing flow of blood, I saw a glint again, but too bright to be metal. Mr. Benson came over and gently wiped away the remaining blood. And there, underneath, was a gold bar cut through my nipple. On either end was a small, glittering diamond. I looked up in wonder at Mr. Benson.

"I guess we're hitched now, asshole," he said.

EPILOGUE

So, Jamie's gone and told you his life story.

I knew the little fucker was up to something. He's been hiding in his little playroom for hours every day, and I've known he's been using the typewriter whenever I left him alone in the apartment.

I don't care that he's written it all down, not at all. It does sort of amuse me to read the result, though. Bottoms are so typical. They inject everything with so much symbolism and so much jargon.

Not that he hasn't told you the truth, at least basically. He's right about the meeting, the training I put him through and the ridiculous mess he got himself into. He's even right when he tells you that this is basically a love story. I'm man enough to admit that I love the little bastard.

Still, some parts of the way he's told you the story amuse me and some others intrigue me. When other people have read his story, they've come to me and asked me for my side. They wanted to know how I felt about it all. It's a little different in some ways. Maybe you'd be interested.

I remember the night I met Jamie in the bar for the first time. I had been seeing a few guys. Well, actually, a lot of guys. They were all good fucks and most of them were decent bottoms. But that night I was dissatisfied with the lot of them. It seemed that they all had some part of themselves that they held on to. They were all just experienced enough with SM and leather that they knew just how to do it, too. They knew the games and they could say the words to fool you into thinking that they were in step with your thinking, but they weren't. Whenever things got too real, they'd back off and there you'd be.

I had decided to change some things around in my life. I was in that bar and there was this cute little cloneboy standing there and acting as though he owned the place. You couldn't help but notice him and the way he was holding court. The pecs were just firm enough to press against his shirt and his ass would have stuck out in any pair of jeans. Nice, I remember thinking, very nice.

I wasn't used to *nice,* though. I was used to *spectacular*. It's easy when you have a rep to get the really show-stopping pieces in a town like New York. They come to you the way an aspiring actor goes to a director at a cocktail party and asks for a tryout. You can get almost anything in this city once the word's out that you're a halfway decent top.

Models, actors, business leaders, porn stars, just about anyone you think is gay and hot is available to a well-known top. Just about anyone. But after a while the bodies blur, no matter that the blur is made up of some of the most perfect male flesh in America. It's still a blur.

There hadn't been a challenge that meant anything to me in years. My cock loved all the attention it was getting. But I knew there had to be something else I wanted.

There was Jamie. Cute ass, nice face, little chest

and he was daring to cruise me. I know when I'm really attracted to someone. When that happens the one thing I really, really want is to storm across the room and smash him one right across the face. That was the visceral response I had that night. I just wanted to slap that little shit … *hard*.

As I stood there and looked at him playing his little clone games my plan started to take shape. Here was a *tabula rasa*. Here was an unformed personality. This was a boy I could take and turn into a man. Just the man I wanted.

It's not my style to ask for what I want. I usually take. But the guy on the other end has to be willing to do the giving. He has to at least have some idea about what he's getting into and some desire to be there. So when Jamie walked over and offered me that first drink I knew I had to start with a test. That's why I had him throw away the underwear. If he had said no or if he had given me any grief I just would have walked away.

You have to understand: It wasn't that my life was bad back then. It wasn't that I was in need of Jamie. I was just looking for a challenge. If he hadn't been able to give it to me or if I hadn't found someone else down there in the Village, I would have just gone back to the clubhouse or up to one of the leather bars and resumed my regular routine. I would have gotten by.

But Jamie did it. He did that and a lot more. He was so anxious and so willing that he kept me on my feet for a good long time. Like I've told you, there were things that happened that were different from my point of view than they were from his. You want some examples?

Beating ass. Beating ass is one of the great pleasures in my life. I don't know why and I don't care. I love the sight of a male body on its hands and knees on the floor in front of me. I love the feel of the skin, whether it's hairless or covered with fuzz, I don't care. I just love the skin. I love the way a bottom's ass quivers when he knows he's going to get the belt.

And I love giving it to him. I like starting off slow and easy, letting him get used to the idea. It was like that with Jamie. I did all the things that I knew he'd need to get through it—the dirty talking and the rough orders. They weren't nearly as important to me as they were to him. I just wanted to watch his ass cheeks.

I started slow, just like I always do. Laying the leather on with almost feathered softness. I watched the whiteness of his virgin ass transformed into a glowing pink. My cock was hard by then, just looking at the wonder of that change. I'd stop every once in a while and touch it, marveling at the warmth that came from my belt's ministrations. I think the way he jumped when he felt the cool of my palm was as erotic as anything else.

I'd take one hand and I'd keep the two halves of his buttocks spread apart and I'd apply the belt vertically so the leather could get at his hole and the cleft that was protected by the mounds. I didn't want any part of his ass to escape the heat of my leather. Not one square inch. Usually bottoms break during a long beating like that one. When I saw that Jamie wasn't going to give in, I knew I had chosen well. The only way a good top can really let himself take the pleasure he wants is when the bottom he's picked has decided that he's going to be defiant. Then you can really go to work.

I did. Not as much as I wanted to, but enough to really enjoy myself. I started to let the belt fly through the air and land with thudding blows that nearly sent him sprawling to his face. I was leaving marks. I knew it and I loved it. I hate the idea of any piece of male flesh leaving my apartment without something to remind the guy about me for the next few days. I love bruises.

I wanted to go much further that night, much further, but I kept some control on myself. I already sensed that this kid was going to be able to learn to take more later on. It was worth holding myself back then. I'd get my just rewards if I simply invested more in him.

Then I put him through his paces. The little humiliations, the verbal demands. Finally, making him sleep on the floor.

While he curled up in that blanket at the foot of my bed, I stayed awake and listened to the little-boy noises he makes while he sleeps and I plotted the next few steps.

That's when the regular sessions began. That's when I started the process that led to him moving in with me. It was all … *all* … carefully thought out.

Some things were done for a psychology that Jamie didn't know existed. Others were done strictly for pleasure and any deep meaning that Jamie put into them was absolutely his own head trip.

Like shaving him. He's nowhere near as tall as I am. His body is much younger. It wasn't all that well developed in those days, but that was okay. He was young enough that there was a natural tone to it. On one level I wanted to accentuate that youthfulness. I wanted to turn him into a boy for a while. On another level I wanted to make him more naked than he had ever been before in his life.

So I shaved him. When I did it something unexpected happened. Like I told you, I can get a spectacular bottom nearly at will in any leather bar you

name. That's easy. I've taken a razor to a lot of them.
I'd put on the cream and I'd spit in their faces and I'd
mind-fuck them with long, lingering strokes of the
blade. But when I shaved Jamie, maybe because of
the things I had been thinking about him, my head
changed around.

I really got into it. I did it carefully and slowly. I'd
take my time shaving—not because I wanted to play
with his mind—but because it occurred to me that
this was going to be mine.

That was a change in my attitude, right there. I
had decided he was going to be a project before, but
then I knew he was going to be a part of my life and
if that was so, I wanted to know every intimate detail.
I wanted to see just how the skin on his balls wrin-
kled. I wanted to know the exact shape of the slit in
his cock. I wanted to feel the precise dimensions of
his nipples. I wanted to gauge the firmness of his
calves and the softness of his ass.

It was, in my mind, as though he were some
strong, healthy young animal on a pedestal and I was
grooming him for show. I was in my own world while
I shaved him. I entered a dimension I had never been
in before.

When I fucked Jamie's hairless body that night it
was with a passion that surpassed any I'd known
before. There was the physical delight of the smooth
body, of course. But it was also with the mental belief
that this was *my* body and that I was going to have
the power and the opportunity to change it just as I
wanted to.

That's when I decided to get him some weights to
work out with. It was an easy connection to decide to
change around his mind as well. It all merged into a
conviction that I was going to make for myself the
best masochistic lover that was ever going to be pos-

sible. I had never found one I had really wanted out there. So I'd create my own.

Of course it was a power trip. So what? You've read what he's said about his life before me. He was a dull, boring twerp, a cipher making his way through life without thought and almost without emotion.

I spent a lot of time thinking about Jamie and about myself after that. He's chosen to see it all in terms of a certain grand design of mine, or of the expected actions of a sex gymnast. It was a little different than that for me.

Like his tits. That night when he was strung up to the wall and he decided that he was going to show me just how much he had, was one of the most beautiful nights we've ever had. It was wonderful. It happened, essentially, just the way he said. By the time he had stopped fighting and crying and twisting and then just stood there and took it, I was ready to fuck him so hard I couldn't find the words to tell you about it.

I just remember I let him down and shoved him onto the floor. I had my cock out and I rammed it into him. He won't admit it, but in the beginning he used to fight that first thrust, the entry of my hard dick into his ass. But that night he opened his *body*. My prick slid in like it belonged there.

It did. I knew it at that very moment. It just went up his hole and his ass gripped it and the feeling of total encasement in Jamie's hot body was mystical, or as close to mystical, as I'll ever experience.

I fucked him for two hours, right on the floor. I kept biting my lip and forcing myself not to shoot. I wanted to have that feeling of possession for the rest of my life. I'd let the head of my cock come right out to the pucker of his hole and I'd keep it there. Then I'd send the whole thing right back up inside him in one long, even motion.

Sometimes, when I thought I could control it, I'd pound him. I'd fuck him as hard as I could, hammering against him until I could feel our pelvic bones grinding against each other. When I came, I came with the yell and the freedom of an animal.

There are lots of things that Jamie sees as sex trips that were more important than that. Much more important, I know about men. I have never denied that a bottom is a male. If he weren't, why'd I want him? But society's fucked up some guys so much that it takes drastic measures to get them out of the shit.

I paid a lot of attention to Jamie's tits. A lot more than one night's worth. There were two reasons. One's obvious. When you're a top you want an easy way to exert control, physical control, over your boy. Sore tits, nipples with last night's work still at play on them, are just about the easiest thing you can do. I like to keep Jamie's tits nice and tender, right at that point where even the flick of a finger can send electric signals shivering through his body.

But there's another level. Jamie had these warped ideas about being intimate. Since I had decided that this one was going to be around for a while, I wanted him to get over that very quickly. Like most other guys, it was easier to get Jamie used to taking the belt than it was getting him to the place where he'd be willing to put his arms around me and lay his head on my shoulder. That delicate submission is sometimes more important to me than any other.

I used Jamie's tits to make him do that. I made his nipples so sore for so long that he would do anything in the world to keep my hands off of them. Anything, including clutching me to him as hard as he could, so hard that there was no room between our bodies, no space for my hands to travel up to his nipples. Jamie would hold me as tightly as he could and hold his head on my neck and beg, *beg* me to hold him. That's how Jamie got used to being close to a man.

He didn't tell you about that because he wants to have you think he took everything just about right, just as much as I gave out. But the closeness, the intimacy, was what really took a lot of work for him. And we used—*I* used—SM to make it happen.

I think tops are misunderstood. It never seems as if anyone wants to take us and what happens to us seriously. Let me try to explain.

It's easy to take an anonymous muscle-bound body out of a bar and to bring him home. You take out the clamps and the hoods and the restraints and the belts and the crops and the blindfolds and all the rest of the contraptions. You do a good job and you're rewarded by getting your rocks off. Fine. But no one ever writes about the cumulative effect of SM. How every time becomes another building block in your respect for a bottom.

That's what happened with me and Jamie. Every trip became another part of the emotional bond between us. Every time I'd present him with a test or an obstacle and he'd get through it, the emotion of my pride would build. It was the constant willingness of his part to work at being worthy of me that created the ever-increasing respect I had for him.

I guess it all climaxed with that stupid rescue scene over in Jersey. *Jersey!* That was a kick in the balls. But, anyway, when I got there and I finally saw that the kid was okay, I was relieved. More than just a little bit, of course; I was so overcome with relief that I had to accept just how important Jamie had become to me. It had all worked; all the dynamics and all the plans had come to a head and there we were, fucking *in love*.

It became necessary for me to have a physical

expression of that love, that's why the tit bars. Well, I also knew they'd just make Jamie's nipples even more sensitive as well, but they were mine and they were on his body. When I licked the little droplets of blood off his chest that night, I felt like we'd had a communion with one another, that we'd made a pact that could never be broken.

Can you stand listening to a sloppy top? Jesus, this is almost embarrassing.

Jamie's book would leave you believing that we still exist in a context of constant and violent SM. I know that every bottom in America would like to believe that. Well, maybe we do from your point of view. It seems to me, given who I am, that we're actually pretty tame now. If you can be tame with a playroom with more toys than are for sale in Folsom Street.

I live my life the same as always. I have my little business dealings and I like to listen to my music. I enjoy good food—I sent Jamie to a chef's school to help in that department. I like to read. And while I sit in my favorite chair I get to see Jamie walking through the apartment and I get the satisfaction of knowing that he's there whenever I want him.

That's the basic rule, the one I won't negotiate. Jamie's ass is mine. I take it when I feel like it. Jamie's mouth is mine. It does what I want when I want. The rest? Well, we can talk about some things, so long as they don't have anything to do with the use of his hole or his face.

Jamie hasn't told you all about his changes. He has a body now. Two hours a day with the weights or in the swimming pool have taken care of that. His nipples are still getting bigger and those tiny diamonds look fine against the dark red of his tits. There's a ring in the head of his cock as well. A gold ring that I can catch ahold of whenever I feel like it.

He has hair back on his body. I'm not sure he likes that, but he hasn't complained. I had gotten him to feel that nakedness he needed. And I had gotten my pleasure out of play-acting that he was a little boy for long enough. When I fuck a hole I want to know it's a man, and that tuft of hair on his chest and the little wisps under his arms and around his cock and balls are pleasant reminders.

There's one thing he doesn't particularly like having back—his underwear. But, hell, there's nothing like a pair of white briefs to help along the fantasy. He keeps complaining that he should be made to wear a dirty jock strap—typical bottom. I want jockey shorts. I get jockey shorts.

I'm intrigued by something that I don't think he understands even now. It's not really in his book. He mentions my rules. One of them is that he can't touch his cock, but I don't think he really knows why. He just talks about it being mine and he shouldn't touch it.

Jamie, like every other bottom, needs to be constantly reminded that he needs his top. He calls me his "master," but sometimes bottoms stray away from their understanding of why and you need something to remind them. There's nothing more powerful as a symbol of the way he needs me than for me to control his orgasm. That's why he can't touch his cock. I know he wouldn't dare do it during the day; at night I make sure his hands are tied to something so he can't reach his groin.

What I do is this: I fuck him at will. I tell him to come over and get on his knees and take out my cock whenever I feel like it. I watch his own tool stiffen and stretch against the restraint of the cotton fabric of his briefs. I don't let him touch it.

I usually wait until it starts to get to him. I can tell.

He'll have blueballs in the morning; the pain will be obvious as he walks across the floor. Or he'll have a hard-on half the day; I can see it in his shorts. The very sound of my voice can make him throw a rod.

That's when I remind him of just how good I am to him. I have him come over and sit on my lap. I suck in the ringed tits and roll them between my teeth. I grab hold of his balls and cup them in my hands, his trust the perfect evidence of our bond. Who else but a perfect lover would you trust to hold your balls like that?

I get him close to the point of tears, sometimes beyond that point. Then I reach into his shorts and drag out his cock. The thing won't have been touched for days and suddenly I'm holding it for him. The kisses come quickly then, they shower over my face and hair. I slowly jerk him off, letting him build up a good head of steam. Every once in a while—just so he doesn't get too cocky about it—I stop then. I send him away. I think Jamie would rather take hours with the belt than to have me do that. The most realistic begging he's ever done has been when I've ended my manipulations of his cock and told him he couldn't have any more.

He gotten down on his knees and kissed my feet with the passion of the possessed.

But usually I do let him come. I jerk him off easily and firmly until the pulsing of his cock sends the streams of come splashing out onto my hand. He licks it up greedily and thankfully. Jamie never forgets how important we are to one another because he knows that I'm the source of his greatest relief. He waits anxiously for those occasional invitations to climb up on my lap and to feel the grip of my palm on his cock.

A top goes through so many stages with a bottom.

Master. Torturer. Drill instructor. Confidant. Instructor. Jamie and I have gotten to know each other so well that he can tell by the tone of my voice which role I'm in and want him to respond to. I can pick up on his needs and be the man he wants.

But it seems to me that we most often come back to one special role. Daddy. It seems to me that I've had a hand in creating this man who is now my slave/lover/brother/possession/recruit/masochist. He wasn't this person before me. He is something more since me. And there, so far as I'm concerned, is the magic of SM. The kid that was Jamie *knew* he had to change and he decided to trust me to change him.

More than that, once he trusted me, I knew I had a set of obligations to be the man he needed. I only have to be the man I want to be with a trick. Once I took on Jamie, I had to do more than that. I guess you could say I was challenged as much by him as he was by me.

Aristotle Benson

ABOUT THE AUTHOR

Mr. Benson is the first of more than thirty-five books written or edited by John Preston. Among his other well-known titles are *Franny the Queen of Provincetown, Hometowns,* and *The Heir* (to be published by Badboy Books in a single volume along with *The King*). John Preston is an accomplished journalist, the former editor of *The Advocate*; his articles and essays have been published in periodicals from *Drummer* to *Harper's,* and from *Interview* to *The Taos Review*. He lives in Portland, Maine.

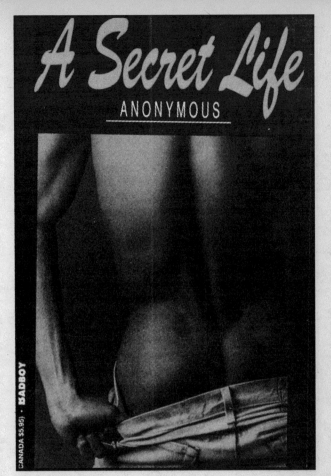

A Secret Life

ANONYMOUS

Meet that remarkably well-set-up young aristocrat, Master Charles Powerscourt: only eighteen, and *quite* innocent ... until his arrival at Sir Percival's Royal Academy, where the daily lessons are supplemented with a crash course in pure, sweet sexual heat! Banned for decades, this exuberant account of gay seduction and initiation is too hot to keep secret any longer!

017-2 **$4.95**

SINS OF THE CITIES OF THE PLAIN

ANONYMOUS · **BADBOY**

(16-4)
US
$4.95

.95 (CANADA $5.95) ·

SINS OF THE CITIES OF THE PLAIN

ANONYMOUS

Indulge yourself in the scorching memoirs of young Eton man-about-town Jack Saul. From his earliest erotic moments with Jerry in the dark of his bedchamber, to his shocking dalliances with the lords and "ladies" of British high (and *very* gay) society, well-endowed Jack's positively *sinful* escapades grow wilder with every chapter! A sensual delight!

016-4 $4.95

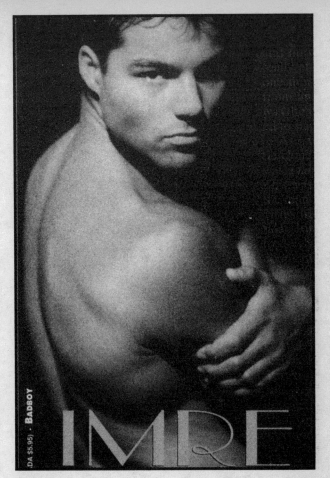

IMRE

W hat dark secrets, what fiery passions lay hidden behind strikingly beautiful Lieutenant Imre's emerald eyes? An extraordinary lost classic of fantasy, obsession, gay erotic desire, and romance in a tiny Austro-Hungarian military town on the eve of WWI. Finally available in a handsome new edition, *Imre* is a potent and dynamic novel of longing and desire.

019-9 **$4.95**

YOUTHFUL DAYS

A hot account of gay love and sex that picks up on the adventures of the four amply-endowed lads last seen in *A Secret Life,* as they lustily explore all the possibilities of homosexual passion. Charlie Powerscourt and his friends cavort on the shores of Devon and in stately Castle Hebworth, then depart for the steamy back streets of Paris. Growing up has never been so hard!

018-0   **$4.95**

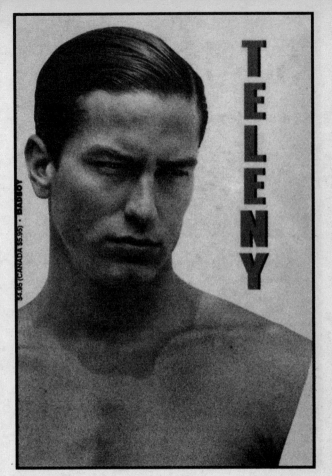

O ften attributed to Oscar Wilde, *Teleny* is a strange,
compelling novel, set amidst the color and deca-
dence of *fin-de-siècle* Parisian society. A young stud
of independent means seeks only a succession of volup-
tuous and forbidden pleasures, but instead finds love and
tragedy when he becomes embroiled in an underground
cult devoted to fulfilling the darkest fantasies.

020-2 $4.95

The Scarlet Pansy

The great American gay camp classic! This is the story of Randall Etrange, a man who simply would not set aside his sexual proclivities and erotic desires during his transcontinental quest for true love, choosing instead to live life to the fullest. Sprawling, melodramatic, and wildly out of control, this novel features scene after scene of incredibly hot gay sex!

021-0

$4.95

MUSCLE BOUND

5 (CANADA $5.95) • BADBOY

In the tough, gritty world of the contemporary New York City bodybuilding scene, country boy Tommy joins forces with sexy, streetwise Will Rodriguez in an escalating battle of wits and biceps at the hottest gym in the West Village. A serious, seething account of power and surrender, in a place where young flesh is firm and hard, and those who can't cut it are bound and crushed at the hands of iron-pumping gods.

028-8 **$4.95**

MEN
AT
WORK

He's the most gorgeous man you have ever seen. You yearn for his touch at night, in your empty bed; but you are a man—and he's your co-worker! Badboy's first anthology is a collection of eight sizzling stories of man-to-man on-the-job training by the hottest authors of gay erotica today. Top cops vie for new blood in *Blue Magnets*, pizza boys enjoy a slice of sex in *The Dough Boys*, and many more!

027-X   **$4.95**

SEXPERT

A collection of
selected columns from
The Advocate Men

EDITED BY
Pat Califia

For many years now, the sophisticated gay man has known that he can turn to one authority for answers to virtually any question on the subject of man-to-man intimacy and sexual performance. Straight from the pages of *Advocate Men* comes The Sexpert! From penis size to toy care, bar behavior to AIDS awareness, The Sexpert responds to real concerns with uncanny wisdom and a razor wit.

034-2   **$4.95**

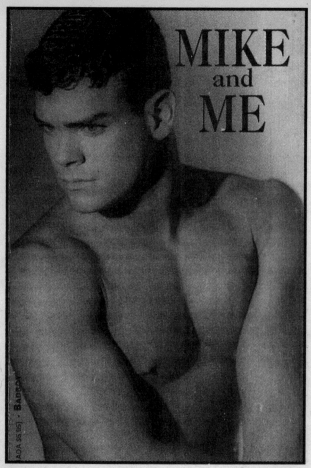

MIKE and ME

Mike joined the gym squad at Edison Community
College to bulk up on muscle and enjoy the com-
petition. Little did he know he'd be turning on
every sexy muscle jock in Southern Minnesota! Hard bodies collide for a series of workouts designed to generate a
whole lot more than rips and cuts. Get ready to hit the
showers with this delicious muscle-boy fantasy romp!

035-0 $4.95

SLOW BURN

CANADA $5.95) • MASQUERADE BOOKS

Welcome to the Body Shoppe, where men's lives cross in the pursuit of muscle. From the authors who brought you BADBOY's *Men at Work* comes a new anthology of heated obsession and erotic indulgence: *Slow Burn.* Torsos get lean and hard, biceps and shoulders grow firm and thick, pecs widen and stomachs ripple in these sexy stories of the power and perils of physical perfection.

042-3 $4.95

THE
HEIR

THE
KING

TWO NOVELS by

John Preston's ground-breaking novel *The Heir*, written in the lyric voice of the ancient myths, tells the story of a world where slaves and masters create a new sexual society. This stylish new edition of the *The Heir* also includes a completely original work called *The King*. This epic tale tells the story of a young soldier who discovers his monarch's most secret desires.

048-2   **$4.95**

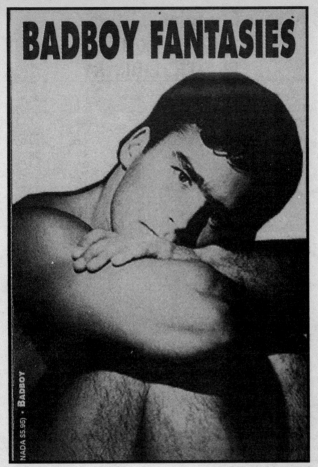

BADBOY FANTASIES

NADA $5.95) · **BADBOY**

When love eludes them—lust will do! They are the rebels, the bikers, the beach boys ... and they couldn't care less about money or politics. Thrill-seeking men caught up in dreams and mysteries—these are the brief encounters that comprise *BADBOY Fantasies*. Guaranteed to get you fantasizing about a BADBOY of your very own!

049-0   **$4.95**

A Complete Listing Of
MASQUERADE'S
EROTIC LIBRARY

Title	Code	Price
CLARA	80-7	$4.95
FORBIDDEN DELIGHTS	81-5	$4.95
DOUBLE NOVEL	86-6	$6.95
LUST	82-3	$4.95
A MASQUERADE READER	84-X	$4.95
THE BOUDOIR	85-8	$4.95
JUDITH BOSTON	87-4	$4.95
SEDUCTIONS	83-1	$4.95
FRAGRANT ABUSES	88-2	$4.95
SCHOOL FOR SIN	89-0	$4.95
CANNIBAL FLOWER	72-6	$4.95
KIDNAP	90-4	$4.95
DEPRAVED ANGELS	92-0	$4.95
ADAM & EVE	93-9	$4.95
THE YELLOW ROOM	96-3	$4.95
AUTOBIOGRAPHY OF A FLEA III	94-7	$4.95
THE SWEETEST FRUIT	95-5	$4.95
THE ICE MAIDEN	3001-6	$4.95
WANDA	3002-4	$4.95
PROFESSIONAL CHARMER	3003-2	$4.95
WAYWARD	3004-0	$4.95
MASTERING MARY SUE	3005-9	$4.95
SLAVE ISLAND	3006-7	$4.95
WILD HEART	3007-5	$4.95
VICE PARK PLACE	3008-3	$4.95
WHITE THIGHS	3009-1	$4.95
THE INSTRUMENTS OF THE PASSION	3010-5	$4.95
THE PRISONER	3011-3	$4.95
OBSESSIONS	3012-1	$4.95
MAN WITH A MAID: The Conclusion	3013-X	$4.95
CAPTIVE MAIDENS	3014-8	$4.95
THE CATALYST	3015-6	$4.95
THE RELUCTANT CAPTIVE	3022-9	$4.95
ALL THE WAY	3023-7	$4.95
CINDERELLA	3024-5	$4.95
THREE WOMEN	3025-3	$4.95
SLAVES OF CAMEROON	3026-1	$4.95
THE VELVET TONGUE	3029-6	$4.95
NAUGHTIER AT NIGHT	3030-X	$4.95
KUNG FU NUNS	3031-8	$4.95
SILK AND STEEL	3032-6	$4.95
THE DISCIPLINE OF ODETTE	3033-4	$4.95
PAULA	3036-9	$4.95
BLUE TANGO	3037-7	$4.95
THE APPLICANT	3038-5	$4.95
SILK AND STEEL	3032-6	$4.95
THE SECRET RECORD	3039-3	$6.95
PROVINCETOWN SUMMER	3040-7	$4.95
A CRUMBLING FACADE	3043-1	$4.95
BLUE VELVET	3046-6	$4.95
DARLING • INNOCENCE	3047-4	$4.95
LOVE IN WARTIME	3044-X	$6.95
DREAM CRUISE	3045-8	$4.95

ORDERING IS EASY!

MC/VISA ORDERS CAN BE PLACED BY CALLING OUR TOLL-FREE NUMBER

1-800-458-9640

OR MAIL THE COUPON BELOW TO:
MASQUERADE BOOKS
801 SECOND AVE.,
NEW YORK, N.Y. 10017

MB 041-5

QTY	TITLE	No.	PRICE
	SUBTOTAL		
	POSTAGE and HANDLING		
	TOTAL		

Add $1.00 Postage and Handling for first book and 50¢ for each additional book. Outside the U.S. add $2.00 for first book, $1.00 for each additional book. New York state residents add 8-1/4% sales tax.

NAME _____

ADDRESS _____ **APT #** _____

CITY _____ **STATE** _____ **ZIP** _____

TEL (___ **)** _____

PAYMENT: ☐ CHECK ☐ MONEY ORDER ☐ VISA ☐ MC

CARD NO. _____ **EXP. DATE** _____

PLEASE ALLOW **4-6 WEEKS** DELIVERY. NO C.O.D. ORDERS. PLEASE MAKE ALL CHECKS PAYABLE TO MASQUERADE BOOKS. PAYABLE IN U.S. CURRENCY ONLY.